KU-492-815

John Creasey
writing as Gordon Ashe

Murder Most Foul

CORGI BOOKS
A DIVISION OF TRANSWORLD PUBLISHERS LTD
A NATIONAL GENERAL COMPANY

MURDER MOST FOUL

A CORGI BOOK 0 552 09286 X

Originally published in Great Britain
by John Long Ltd.

PRINTING HISTORY
John Long edition published 1941
Corgi revised edition published 1973

Copyright © John Creasey 1941
This revised edition copyright © John Creasey 1973

This book is set in Monotype Baskerville

Corgi Books are published by Transworld Publishers Ltd.,
Cavendish House, 57–59 Uxbridge Road,
Ealing, London, W.5.
Made and printed in Great Britain by
Hunt Barnard Printing Ltd., Aylesbury, Bucks.

**NOTE: The Australian price appearing on the back
cover is the recommended retail price.**

314

His name is

PATRICK DAWLISH

He is a very large man, with vast shoulders
that his well-cut suit cannot conceal. But for
the broken nose, a legacy of an early battle
in the boxing ring, he would be as handsome
as he is massive. . . .

He is always jumping in with both feet where
the police fear to tread. And no thief,
blackmailer or murderer ever comes up
against a tougher, more resourceful, deadlier
enemy than

PATRICK DAWLISH

MURDER MOST FOUL, one of the
Patrick Dawlish series, is by John Creasey
writing as Gordon Ashe, of which there are
now over forty titles and many have been
published by Corgi Books.

Born in 1908, John Creasey died in June 1973.
Overall, his books have sold nearly a hundred
million copies and have been translated into
28 languages.

As well as travelling extensively, he had a
particular interest in politics and was the
founder of *All Party Alliance*, which advocates
a new system of government by the best
candidates from all parties and independents.
He fought in five parliamentary by-elections
for the movement.

Also by JOHN CREASEY

and published by CORGI BOOKS

Murder Most Foul

CHAPTER I

Captain Dawlish is Amiable

A tall, thin man dressed in a faultless lounge suit drove a Lagonda car into the carriage-way of Marsham Lodge. So black and shiny was the Lagonda that the September sun reflected from it and dazzled the eyes of a large man who stood idly on the steps of the front entrance.

The newcomer alighted, then helped out his companion, a girl who appeared to be in her early twenties. She flashed him a dazzling smile, and murmured an endearment.

With arms linked, the couple approached the steps.

The large man sauntered towards them. He was not in keeping with the imposing appearance of the Lodge, for his flannels were baggy, and his khaki shirt open at the neck. Certainly there was no touch of affluence about him, but nor, to the discerning eye, did he look like a porter.

Nevertheless, the newcomer said casually:

'Bring in my luggage, and put the car away.'

Ignoring the larger man's raised eyebrows he strode through the hall to the reception desk. A middle-aged woman received them pleasantly.

'My name is Black – Raymond Black. I wired for accommodation.'

'Oh, yes, Mr Black. I will have you shown to your rooms. If you will wait just a moment I will ring for a maid.'

They stood waiting, and then the revolving doors opened, and the large man entered. In either hand he carried a suitcase; under each arm he carried a smaller one. A man of normal size would have appeared dwarfed by the baggage, but this one did not look over-burdened.

The receptionist turned about.

'If you will sign the registration forms when you get to your rooms, sir, and send them down, I would be – '

She stopped, and what she would be was not disclosed, for she had seen the large man with his burdens. Her mouth dropped open a little, and she gulped. Then:

'Mr – Mr *Dawlish* – '

For the first time Black took some interest in the untidy giant, and frowned.

'Aren't you the porter?'

'Porter!' exclaimed the receptionist. 'No, Mr Dawlish certainly *isn't!* Please put the cases down, sir, and I'll send for Frederick immediately.'

Mr Dawlish smiled; it was a friendly smile.

'Oh, I can finish it now I've started, and Frederick's busy this afternoon.' He regarded Mr and – presumably – Mrs Black. 'Everywhere's understaffed, of course, and they're not finding it easy to carry on.'

The receptionist clearly wished that he would change his mind, but Dawlish insisted. Black smiled, a thin-lipped and half-amused smile, and then the maid appeared to take him to the rooms. Arriving, Black looked round disparagingly.

'Can't you do better than this?'

The maid shook her head. 'We're full *right* up, sir.'

'I wired for two large rooms,' said Black. 'Send the manager to me as soon as you've finished here.' He stepped to the bedroom in which was a large double-bed, and his frown grew ominous. 'No, this is too bad. I ordered single beds.'

'I'm sorry, sir.'

'Send the manager to me at once,' said Black, and turned to Dawlish, whom apparently he had forgotten. 'Oh. Would you mind putting them by the door? I don't propose to stay here.'

Dawlish smiled.

'Too bad. There isn't another decent pub inside twenty miles.'

'I'm not suggesting I should move from the Lodge,' said Black, 'but they must find me better accommodation. Eileen, you've got a smut on your right cheek.'

Quietly Dawlish withdrew, meeting Pierpont, the Lodge's manager, in the passage. He was a short man, portly, dignified and august. He had been the manager of one of London's exclusive hotels until it had been made useless by bombing; then he had invested in Marsham Lodge, a Hampshire country house which had been empty for some years. He had spent liberally, and finally he had announced through the columns of the *Times*, that Marsham Lodge, under the management of Pierre Pierpont, had opened as a country hotel near the New Forest, that it had every modern amenity, and that it offered freedom from the terrors of the air.

It had been open for six months; and it was proving very popular.

Dawlish sauntered down the stairs, and out into the garden. A short, stumpy man was wrestling with a hoe; he commented sourly, and at length, on weeds and their fecundity.

'You should be grateful, Frederick,' declared Dawlish.

'For what?' demanded Frederick, an aggressive man who had learned that Mr Dawlish was a safe recipient of confidences and complaints.

'Well, you're in comparative safety – a good job – '

'Gimme London,' said Frederick. 'You can keep the country, gimme London. If it 'adn't been for 'er – '

He went on to say that if his wife, who clearly exerted a considerable influence on him, had not been so stubborn, he would have stayed in London, where he had been born and bred, and where his heart remained.

Dawlish waved a sympathetic hand, and went on.

Near the road, the flower-garden gave way to shrubbery, and he walked through it. In a very few minutes he came to a summer-house. There a tall, slim girl was sitting in a deck-chair talking to Timothy Jeremy, a very old friend of Dawlish's. He was in uniform, three pips on his shoulder.

9

Dawlish surveyed them both with humour, then took out a cigarette case.

'Before you smoke, tell us what happened,' said the girl, whose name was Felicity and who had been engaged to Dawlish for nearly two years.

'Has he arrived?' asked Jeremy.

'Yes, they've arrived.'

'*They?*' Felicity repeated. 'Are there *two* of them?'

'And not only that,' said Dawlish. 'You are no longer the belle of the Lodge, my sweet.'

'Oh-ho. The mystery thickens,' said Jeremy.

'Deepens,' corrected Dawlish, joining Jeremy on the grass and sitting cross-legged. 'Only plots thicken. She's a pretty wench indeed, and don't squint, Felicity! He's – well, he's sleek and smooth and unmannerly. *Her* name is Eileen – '

'You've been very successful – so far,' said Felicity coolly.

'Yes, haven't I?' Dawlish told them just what had happened, and smiled at their indignant reaction. Then he frowned.

'So now we've made one move forward. He isn't an easy customer to sum up, but if he has one weakness, I should say it was vanity. I suppose it *is* worth spending our time down here? There are better places, and Crummy might be crazy.'

'Even if there are, and he is, surely it's a relief just to do nothing,' Felicity murmured.

Dawlish smiled. 'I do a lot of that when I'm not on leave,' he said. 'The trouble with the civilian population is that they don't appreciate the extent of a poor soldier's boredom. However, if there are better places, there are certainly worse ones, so come what may we'll stay.'

'Lucky dog,' said Jeremy. 'I must be off early in the morning. What's the time?'

Dawlish glanced at his watch. 'Half-past five.'

'Supposing we stay here for half-an-hour, and then go for a drink?' suggested Jeremy. 'The weather's the thirstiest I've known this year. But I remember once – '

'Oh *no!*' breathed Dawlish.

'It was in July,' Jeremy went on imperturbably, 'and you know what the Scottish moors are like. They stretch for miles. Well, we started at dawn, and – Pat, drat you, are you listening?'

Dawlish was looking away from Jeremy. He was quite motionless. He said in an undertone:

'Yes, go on you idiot.'

Jeremy went on.

Felicity said quietly:

'What is it, Pat?'

'A pair of legs where they shouldn't be.'

Dawlish's utter stillness was a strange thing, yet it did not surprise Jeremy or Felicity.

They knew Dawlish better, perhaps, than he knew himself.

Only as spectators could they know and fully appreciate the peculiar qualities of the man, his motionlessness when he wanted to be still, the startling speed of his movements when he felt the need for haste.

There were others who knew of Dawlish, and the reputation which, he insisted, had been forced upon him. He considered himself an ordinary man, and except on occasions that was true. Primarily the occasions had been brought to light when he had worked, at first unwillingly, in co-operation with the police. He had followed that up with four 'adventures' – during each of which his uncanny capacity for mingling action with speed of thought had amazed a great many people. But when the affairs were over, he slipped back into his own conception of himself, that of an ordinary man who insisted that his reputation was both unearned and unwelcome.

Now Dawlish, who had, in fact, been waiting to see Raymond Black, peered through the shrubs. His eyes being on a lower level than either of the others – for he was sitting cross-legged on the grass – he could see what was hidden to them.

Presently, they too lowered their gaze to the point at which Dawlish was staring.

The legs belonged, presumably, to a man, for they were trouser-clad. The feet were contained in patent-leather shoes, and were almost as remarkable as Dawlish for their stillness. Then, suddenly, they moved.

Slowly at first, making no sound, as they carried their owner towards the Lodge. Dawlish straightened up, hidden from the man by the width of the trees. He raised a hand to the others enjoining them to silence, and then began to track the movements of the patent-leather shoes.

CHAPTER 2

Patent-Leather Shoes

Dawlish slipped between two shrubs, making no sound, although they pressed against him as he moved. Felicity and Tim tried to repeat the large man's performance, but branches stuck in their faces, caught at their clothes, and forced them to a standstill. They preferred to repress their curiosity until later, when all, or nearly all, would be revealed to them, in greater comfort.

Dawlish reached the spot where he had seen the shoes.

At that point earth replaced the grass, and the shrubs were not so thick. He saw the footprints of the patent-leather wearer, a single track which stopped where Dawlish was standing; there they had made a deeper impression. Then apparently the wearer had been undecided, for a confusion of prints suggested that he had started to go one way, and finally decided on another.

The prints continued towards the rear of the Lodge.

They were easy enough to follow, though the motive of such a furtive reconnaissance of the Lodge was not. Dawlish found himself facing the west wing of the big house. It was here the Blacks had their room.

A window on the first floor was wide open, and he could see two people moving inside the room. He could not at first identify them, then the woman who had accompanied Black, came further into sight. At a distance she was beautiful, for distance hid her defects, and also the fact that she depended rather more on cosmetics than a girl of twenty-odd should do.

Black was not visible.

The girl moved back after a few seconds, while Dawlish, keeping low for he was afraid that he might be seen, contrived to follow the tracks. It was not long before he reached the end of the shrubbery, from there they disappeared into a small copse of trees.

Dawlish followed them, walking nonchalantly and even pausing to look at some foxgloves which had seeded themselves in the grass. Nevertheless he reached the trees in time to see the shoes again. They were making their way towards the Lodge by a narrow path which led to a side entrance, and also to the kitchen garden.

For the first time their wearer was fully visible to Dawlish – a small, natty little man, dark-haired and sleek, olive-skinned and the possessor of hot brown eyes. The eyes of a Spaniard, in fact – or so Dawlish had reflected when he had first glimpsed the man at the Lodge, and learnt that his unlikely name was Smith.

He was now sauntering along the path, and having cast three sharp glances over his shoulder, disappeared into the side entrance of the hall.

Dawlish retraced his own steps to the summer-house, where Felicity and Tim were waiting eagerly.

'Well?' said Tim.

'Who?' asked Felicity.

'Smith,' said Dawlish.

Felicity said: 'But why should he be *there*? I mean why shouldn't he?' She considered her fiance critically. 'Pat, was there any reason for following him? After all, he's a visitor, and he's as much right to be in the shrubbery as you have.'

'Oh it isn't a question of right,' said Dawlish slowly, 'but probability. If you were wearing dress shoes, would you deliberately walk across a shrubbery and get them dirty? Or would you stay on the grass? And even if you decided to be childish, and walked through dirt for the sake of it, would you stand quite still, looking in one direction, for a period not more than ten minutes but certainly not less than five? Smith's presence there was odd; because,' he added thoughtfully, 'it wasn't reasonable. It would have been odd even had he not chosen a position from which he could watch Raymond Black's room.'

Felicity gave a very profound 'ha!' while Jeremy frowned. 'By George, that's queer! Crummy mightn't have been talking bilge after all.'

'Crummy at least made us curious,' said Dawlish.

He considered, silently, the man who was known to his friends – and they were many – as Crummy. The origin of the nickname was simply. In his youth Peter Anson Wise had been much given to saying: 'Oh, crumbs!' Instead of losing the habit in his later schooldays, he had developed it, and even at that time – he was twenty-seven – he would occasionally burst out with the expression when a stronger expletive might have been expected.

Thus 'Crummy' Wise.

An amiable youth, neither good-looking nor bad. A man with a passion for cricket, an eye for a pretty face, generous, reasonably wealthy, he was good company and well-meaning. In the days before the war he had often been called a young idiot, a prime example of the decadent twentieth century, a pleasure-loving nonentity – all the things, in fact, that a young man-about-town would be called by people who disapproved of those who did not work for a living.

The war came, and Crummy was awarded the Military Cross for outstanding bravery.

He had stayed in London during the earlier stages of the blitz, and while showing the same coolness and the same courage, had been badly wounded. It was in the final stages of his convalescence that Dawlish had seen him. Dawlish had reached London on a spell of leave, his first since the Spring, when he had been engaged in the astonishing affair of Sebastian Shaw.*

To Dawlish, whom he knew well, Crummy Wise had unburdened himself.

'I wouldn't shoot this at anyone else, Pat, they'd call me crazy. But it's an odd show – positively. You see that fellow

* Read *Ware Danger*, by Gordon Ashe.

over there? The painfully thin customer whose hair looks as if it's been set in a plaster cast?'

'Yes,' said Dawlish. (They had been sitting in the foyer of a London hotel.)

'I could swear he's the cove I saw in Berlin in '38,' said Crummy. 'I suppose I could be wrong, but he was at the Osterlitz, you know. He had a beautiful girl with him, and when I say beautiful I mean it.'

Dawlish raised an eyebrow.

'Well, why not? And why shouldn't he have been in Berlin? You were.'

'Oh, crumbs!' exclaimed Crummy. 'I didn't tell you, did I? He was with a mob of Luftwaffe men. He was in uniform too – I couldn't be sure what one, they nearly all wear something or other over there. I – well I'm damned, there she is. The beauty, I mean.'

A woman had gone across the foyer and joined the thin man. A woman of thirty-five, if not more, but well-preserved and, if a man liked a mature and sophisticated lovely, then she could not be bettered.

'Well, there it is,' said Crummy. 'I can't be *sure* it's the same fellow, I didn't see him at close quarters, but the likeness – it's astonishing. Positively. Oh, crumbs, I must be off. Promised the mater I'd see her at lunch. What do you think of it – tell me tonight, will you?'

Most men would have been curious. Some would have decided that Crummy was talking nonsense, and had mistaken the man. Others, from sheer indolence of nature, would have forgotten about it. Others again would have considered telling the police, then decided not to risk making fools of themselves. A few, a very few, would have shown a personal interest in the thin man with the dark, waved hair, which was precisely what Dawlish had done.

Moreover he had learned that Black was proposing to go to Marsham Lodge. Since Dawlish had known Pierpont for many years, and had already visited the country hotel, he had obtained rooms for himself and Felicity and Tim without much trouble, and had arrived the previous night.

They arrived precisely six hours after he had discovered that Black had wired for rooms; Dawlish was not a slow moving man. Moreover he had arranged with a friend, one Edward Beresford, who was also on leave, to keep an eye on Black the previous afternoon, evening and – as far as possible – night.

Two hours before Black's arrival, Dawlish had received a telegram:

'Everything went off as arranged no hitch nothing unexpected be good watch your step I'll try to get down for a couple of days Ted.'

So Dawlish had been waiting, and had seen only one thing to surprise him – the girl. It was not the woman he had seen on the previous night, although both were fair. Presumably, since they were sharing the rooms, this one was Black's wife.

Dawlish knew nothing more than that, nothing more than Crummy had told him, but he hoped that he would learn more. It was, he admitted, a cheering thing to happen on leave, for he had found a year and more in the Home Defence Army less active than might have been expected; even at times, positively boring. Also, as Felicity had pointed out, his was a mind which operated with full effectiveness only when there was something unusual to occupy it.

He had told Felicity and Tim everything, of course; and now they sat by the summer-house, wondering why Mr Smith, who looked so Spanish, should be so interested in Mr Black – for interested he must be, otherwise why stare so persistently through his window?

'What are you going to do now?' inquired Tim.

'Continue to be amiable,' said Dawlish cheerfully, 'and keep my weather-eye open. It's about time for that drink, I think.' He hauled himself to his feet, linked arms with Felicity, and walked towards the Lodge, Tim Jeremy doing the same on Felicity's other side. A casual passer-by would have seen them as an idle, presentable trio – presentable, that was, as far as faces were concerned, for only Felicity looked as if her dress had been made for her. She would have looked equally attractive had her clothes been as unconventional as those worn by Dawlish and Tim, for she was exceedingly pretty, and possessed the gift of adding distinction to what she wore. At heart, she disagreed with Dawlish on one thing; she thought they should be married, whereas he considered that it would be wiser to wait until after the war.

She saw the point of his argument, and did not press hers.

They had reached the steps of the Lodge when they heard a cry. It mingled surprise with alarm, Dawlish thought, and it came from the shrubbery they had just left. The sound of heavy footsteps followed the cry, and then the stocky form of Frederick burst from the shrubbery; the man was moving very fast and his face was aglow with excitement and alarm.

Dawlish reached him, and grabbed his arm.

'What – '

'Lemme go, lemme go!' cried Frederick, not a little breathlessly. 'There's bin a murder!'

CHAPTER 3

Not Nice To See

Dawlish's grip on the porter's arm tightened, and he spoke sharply.

'Don't lose your head, man. And don't alarm the whole hotel – if there's trouble, keep it as quiet as you can. Do you want to be fired?'

' 'oo cares about being fired?' demanded Frederick with a fine show of truculence. 'She would 'ave to let me go back to London then. She didn't count on murder, coming down 'ere. I see it meself, with me own eyes. Proper turned me up!'

'What, and where?' asked Dawlish.

'A cove's lying near the road, blimey! they didn't 'arf make a mess of him. Proper turned me up,' Fred repeated, and then he began to realise that perhaps he had talked too much and too loudly.

Dawlish said quietly: 'Go and report to Mr Pierpont at once, Fred – I'll see what I can find. Which is the quickest way to it?'

'Past the summer-'ouse, sir, and straight on.'

There were several people watching them curiously, and half-a-dozen windows were open. Dawlish waited for the porter to go inside, and then turned with the others and hurried back to the summer-house. Beyond it, leading to the second-class road which served the Lodge, there was a winding path.

He would have liked Felicity to stay behind, but knew her too well to suggest it.

He was on edge, for he badly wanted to know who had

been killed. It was possible, of course, that Fred had let his boredom run away with him, and the body was that of a victim of an accident.

It did not take Dawlish long, however, to find this last supposition incorrect. The body lay between the hedge bordering the road, and the first patch of shrubs. It was that of a small man, whose head had been knocked about badly, so that it was not nice to see. He was quite dead. His face, untouched by whatever weapon had bludgeoned him to death, held an expression of surprise; his eyes were wide open, staring sightlessly.

His skin was swarthy, and his name – according to what he had said at the Lodge – was Mr Smith.

Patent-leather shoes, plastered with the earth of the shrubbery, poked towards the road.

*

Dawlish straightened up, and said in a low-pitched voice:

'Nasty show, I'm afraid. Have a look in the road, just in case anyone's about, and you might see if you can find a hammer or anything that could have caused the damage. If you find it, don't touch it or the police will want to know why.'

They obeyed him without question, and Dawlish went down on one knee again. Quickly he withdrew the contents of Smith's breast-pocket, and glanced through them. He saw nothing of interest, unless it was a visiting card, which said:

Stephen Jose Smith,
11, Vere Court, W.1.

Apart from that, there were only a few pound notes and fivers, a time-table, a first-class return ticket to London, a driving licence, registration and identity cards, stamps, and three letter-cards.

Dawlish was fully aware that he was rendering himself liable to reprimand from the police, yet he was puzzled and he wondered whether the murder would be easily solved.

Had he been asked he would have said that he wanted no part in solving it, but that would have been only half-true.

He found nothing of interest in the other pockets, and he could make no further inspection without disturbing the body.

He looked around the spot where the body lay. The turf, just there, was hard, and unlikely to show any footprints. He frowned, left the body, and joined the others. They were together in the road, and they reported that they had seen nothing of interest. Dawlish looked down at the dust and granite chippings thrown to the side after the re-surfacing, which had been done not long before. In the fine dust there were tyre-tracks, just distinguishable; at one point it looked as if a car had started up, and the wheels had at first refused to grip.

'What have you found, Sherlock?' demanded Tim.

'I don't know,' said Dawlish. 'I do know these tracks mustn't be disturbed, and you're going thirsty for a while longer, Tim. But the police shouldn't be long.' He explained why he thought that the patch of dust and chippings should be undisturbed, and Jeremy agreed to keep watch. Dawlish and Felicity walked back to the Lodge.

In the shrubbery his arm was tight about her waist.

'It's not good, darling.'

'It's beastly, but we've seen worse,' said Felicity slowly. 'I suppose I'm getting innured to injuries, Pat, but – why, why must this happen just when you're here?'

Dawlish increased the pressure of his arm.

'Easy, my sweet. It might fizzle out – '

'You don't really think that. Things don't fizzle out with you.'

Dawlish tried to look a good deal more contrite than he was feeling.

'Darling, we're not going to get any further ahead by arguing about that at the moment. We'll have a drink as soon as we get in, that'll steady you. There's nothing to associate me with Smith, no reason why I should be involved.'

'No reason? Do you think you'll be satisfied until you've

found out who killed him, and why? Whether Black had anything to do with it, and why? Do you think – '

She paused, and Dawlish said:

'Do you think you'd really like me to stand by and do nothing?'

'Yes, I would. It's not your job. Pat – ' She stopped still. 'Look at me, and listen. When we met, it was in a beastly business where every moment I was afraid of hearing that you'd been killed. It was worse during the Shaw affair. In both I was stretched to breaking point. I don't think I can stand it again. Don't take any part in this. We've five days left together, let's get away from here when you've made your report – tell the police what Crummy said, tell them everything and then let's get away.'

Slowly Dawlish rubbed the back of his neck.

'On the whole, I'd like to; but whether I'll be allowed to is a different matter.' He looked away from her, and they began to walk forward again. 'Sweet, putting up with me is no sinecure, and well I know it! But there's something bred in me that I can't overcome. I admit that I would like to know all about Smith and Black, if they're associated, and who killed Smith. But I'd also like to have the best part of a week with you, doing nothing in particular, just lazing around, bathing a bit, swimming, walking, playing tennis. A week when we can forget war and all about it, ignore intrigue and murder – yes, I'd like it! So I'll give the police the full story, and if we can get away, we will.'

'If?' she said.

'Well – '

She laughed a little.

'Pat, you're cleverer than I realised – you're bursting to get your hooks in this affair, and you want to make it look as if you'd rather not.'

He kissed her. 'Cross my heart, I'll try to get out of it!' Arm in arm they continued on their way to the Lodge, Dawlish reflecting as he walked that he had tried to tell Felicity just what he felt about the business. Already one half of his mind was busily turning over what Crummy had said.

There was the possibility that Black had known he was being watched, and had taken precautions to prevent it. There were other things, too.

Smith had, ostensibly, returned to the house, but within twenty minutes he had left it again, gone back to the shrubbery and been attacked by someone who had drawn up in a car near the Lodge grounds. That was obvious. What wasn't obvious was Smith's reason for returning to the Lodge and then doubling back.

Had he gone to meet the man who had killed him? or had the encounter been one of complete surprise?

They were the questions in the one half of his mind.

In the other was something near a longing for a quiet spell with Felicity, a holiday while the good weather lasted, a period when there would at least be peace in their hearts, even with war about them.

That word of the murder had already spread about was obvious from the number of people gathered in the foyer. Dawlish and Felicity walked through as if they knew nothing. They had two rooms on the first floor – Dawlish and Jeremy were sharing one, Felicity was in the other on the opposite side of the corridor.

Meeting Black at the top of the stairs he paused and half-turned.

'What is all the excitement about, do you know?'

'It wouldn't surprise me if the gardener hadn't had a fit,' Dawlish said solemnly.

'Why don't you admit that you don't know?' demanded Black testily, and he walked on.

Felicity laughed and shrugged her shoulders. Dawlish frowned.

'Black's way of speaking is strangely reminiscent,' he said. 'The manner of men born, bred and trained to the belief that no one but their own peculiar kind have a right to live on God's good earth.' He paused, and looked at her with one eyebrow raised a little above the other. 'In short, I mean it's German.'

Felicity nodded.

'Yes, I can see that. And it suggests that Crummy was right.'

'It suggests that Mr Raymond Black could well have been in Berlin three years ago, dressed in one of the hybrid uniforms, and consorting with the Luftwaffe.' He laughed a little. 'Should I report observations as well as facts to the police, my sweet?'

'I don't know what to say,' admitted Felicity.

'It's a puzzle, isn't it? You're as undecided as I am. Anyhow, I'll go and change before the police arrive, and then we can have that drink.' He opened her door, and she went in, clasping his hand for a moment before she did so. Smiling and yet thoughtful, trying to sort out the confusion of his mind – a confusion mirrored, he now gathered, in Felicity's – he went into his own room.

He saw nothing surprising in it.

The window was open, but he rarely closed it completely, no matter where he was nor what the weather decided to do. He washed, brushed his hair, and stepped to the wardrobe. It did not open immediately, and he was forced to turn the key. Normally he did not keep it locked – what valuables he had with him were in his valise, and the key of that he kept in his pocket. He frowned, pulled the door open, and then stared.

The wardrobe was nearly empty.

On the shelves were shirts, socks, ties and handkerchiefs, and all the minor accessories. But there was nothing on the hangers, and he stared somewhat stupidly at the first, on which was printed the name and address of his Saville Row tailor. Then his mind clicked into working order.

His uniform was gone.

Tunic – trousers – and greatcoat. They had been in the wardrobe not three hours before, and now they were missing. He glanced at the foot of the wardrobe, and saw with consternation that his service respirator, his Sam Browne belt, and his revolver, had also gone.

CHAPTER 4

Stolen or Borrowed?

'It isn't my eyesight and it isn't my fancy,' said Dawlish, who had wrapped a dressing-gown about him and then gone across to Felicity's room. 'They've gone.'

'But – '

'No time for buts,' said Dawlish. 'I've telephoned for the maid on this floor, as there isn't a chance of seeing Pierpont until the police have arrived, and – oh, here she is. May, do you know where my uniform is?'

May, middle-aged and stout, stared at him with eyes long used to the vagaries of hotel guests.

'*Uniform*, sir?'

'You haven't taken it for pressing?'

'That I haven't, sir. I've enough to do without pressing uniforms, we're everso understaffed, not that I wouldn't if you really wanted it done. Did you say it had gone?'

'Ye-es. May, what do you think of the rest of the staff here?'

May tossed her head. 'A lot o' good-for-nothings, that's what I think. Fresh from school, most of them. Taking advantage of the war, that's what they're doing, knowing the Boss can't sack them 'cos he can't get anyone else.'

'I don't want them to know that this stuff has gone,' Dawlish said quietly.

'Then they won't know from *me*, sir.'

'That's fine,' said Dawlish. 'It's probably a practical joke – Captain Jeremy will have them in his room, I expect.'

'Joke!' repeated May, lugubriously. 'Is there anything more, sir?'

'Not now,' said Dawlish.

She closed the door, and Dawlish eyed Felicity.

'There was just a chance that she'd taken them, but I didn't feel hopeful about it. Well, they've vanished, and so I'll have to get back in my slacks. I wonder – '

'I suppose Tim didn't take them?'

'It isn't likely, but I'll ask him.'

Timothy arrived a few minutes afterwards. The police had seen him standing in the road, and he had left one of them watching the spot until the arrival of the Inspector who, it seemed, was coming from another direction. Two plainclothes men, said Timothy, were in the foyer, and the guests were already becoming curious.

'Pierpont should tell them what's the matter,' said Dawlish. 'Tim, what have you done with my uniform?'

'Uniform?'

'It's gone.'

Tim's expression showed a growing interest.

'Lost, stolen, or borrowed?' he demanded. 'Good lord, one can't leave a thing about, these days.' He lit a cigarette, and then said sharply: 'I say, Pat. Do you think it's connected?'

'To what?' asked Dawlish.

'Well, your uniform's disappeared, and Smith's been murdered. Could be a tie-up.'

'I suppose you're going to tell me that whoever stole my clobber put it on, killed Smith, and then got away with it,' said Dawlish witheringly. 'Don't be an idiot. There's no reason for thinking they might be connected, but it *is* another queer thing. I should have brought some spares with me. Oh, well, they left me a clean shirt if nothing else.'

He was back in his slacks when there was a tap at the door, and a maid whom he had not previously seen asked him if he would mind going to the manager's office.

'Yes, I'll go at once,' he said. But before going he asked Tim to watch Felicity's door.

'What on earth for?'

'I don't know, but I feel it should be done,' said Dawlish.

'People who shouldn't are wandering about, aren't they? Smith wandered into unexpected places, and it didn't do any good. Oh, well, I'd better get downstairs.'

Tim frowned.

'Old boy, I don't think you're quite yourself.'

'I'm sure I'm not,' said Dawlish over his shoulder. He knew of no definite reason why he wanted Felicity's door watched. The suggestion had come instinctively, and only Tim's surprise made him wonder what had inspired it. In a worried and puzzled frame of mind he went downstairs to the manager's office. He found Pierpont in close conversation with two other men.

'Good-evening, Mr Dawlish.' His English was flawless, and held only the slightest trace of accent; Dawlish had heard somewhere that he had spent the last thirty years of his life in England, and knew that he had been naturalised for a long time. 'I am sorry to inconvenience you, but it appears that you can be of some assistance to the police in this distressing matter. Inspector Woodley, this is Captain Dawlish.'

Dawlish regarded a tall, lean-faced man in a brown tweed suit.

'How d'you do, Mr Dawlish. This is my sergeant – ' he motioned to a bulky man sitting by a desk with a notebook open in front of him. 'I hope you can explain a little more fully what happened. The gardener's account is rather vague.'

Dawlish nodded.

'He had a shock, I think. I can tell you what happened from the time I saw him, of course.' He plunged into his narrative, making it brisk and brief, but leaving out no essential – unless his vague suspicions of Black, the loss of the uniform, and his earlier sight of Smith in the shrubbery were essentials; he did not think they were, just then.

When he had finished, Woodley nodded.

'That's very concise, sir. Now I believe you arranged for the road to be watched – will you explain why?'

'I saw the marks of a car near the spot where Smith was

found, said Dawlish. 'It might mean nothing, it might mean a lot. I thought it wise to make sure the marks weren't disturbed.'

'Thank you.' Woodley eyed him curiously. 'I think – ' he stopped abruptly, and his eyes widened. 'Surely you are not the Captain Dawlish connected with the Shaw affair earlier in the year?'

Dawlish lifted his hands.

'I'm afraid so.'

'That explains a lot!' said Woodley. 'I thought there was a practised air about your report. I'm very glad of the opportunity of meeting you. Er – how much leave have you left?'

Dawlish smiled. 'A few days, and I'd like them quiet!'

'Quite so,' said Woodley, but his expression belied his words. 'If you'd care to come with me while I look at the road and the body – I've had no time for more than a cursory examination, yet, and the surgeon should be there by now.'

Dawlish said: 'Do you mind if I don't? I've been there once, and there isn't anything I can do that you won't be able to handle much more efficiently.' His smile was disarming. 'Spare me hard work, Inspector!'

'Just as you like,' said Woodley.

'Thanks very much. There *is* one other odd thing – ' he decided that it would be wise to mention the missing uniform. Pierpont, however, was far more worried than the Inspector, and when the police had left the office he regarded Dawlish with some anxiety.

'Mr Dawlish, I do most sincerely apologise for the inconvenience the theft will cause you. If there is any way I can help I am at your service.'

'If you can find the beggar who took it, or even get it back, it would be a help,' said Dawlish. 'But you've more on your mind than a disappearing uniform at the moment.'

'Well, that is so of course. A nasty business. I propose to make a formal statement at dinner – in half-an-hour's time,' said Pierpont. 'I shall have the opportunity of taking the police advice, then.'

'Ye-es. I shouldn't leave it any longer,' said Dawlish. 'They'll start chattering, you know – '

He stepped to the door and opened it, and as he did so he heard a sharp intake of breath on the other side. When he looked through, he saw Black, standing unnecessarily close.

Dawlish eyed him curiously, sure that the man wore a wig.

Black stood aside, but before Dawlish had passed, he said:

'Is there no end to the inconvenience here? I have been ringing for a maid for the last ten minutes.'

There was a sharp edge to Pierpont's voice as he answered:

'You must please make allowances, Mr Black, for the shortage of staff – '

'But this is too much. There's no hot water in the taps – '

'Will you kindly close the door?' said Pierpont coldly. Dawlish went on, sorry that he had not heard the rest of that interchange. As it happened, he was at the end of the passage talking to Tim, who was waiting for his drink and near whom Felicity was standing talking to a hotel acquaintance, when Black left the office.

Black did not look pleased. In fact his cheeks were flushed and his eyes glittering as he passed. Tim Jeremy screwed up his homely face at sight of him. A plain man, Jeremy, yet one whom most people instinctively liked.

'One nose out of joint,' he murmured, 'and I can't say I'm sorry. Anyhow, I'm thirsty – who's for a drink?' He led the way to the American bar and gave a quick order.

'Well, what's happened?' Felicity asked.

'The policeman's name is Woodley, and I fancy he would like me to be more interested than I am,' said Dawlish. 'Apart from that, nothing as far as I know. Except, of course, that Black was listening at the door when I talked with Pierpont.'

'*Was* he, by George! Crafty customer.' Tim finished his beer and eyed the empty tankard thoughtfully. He waited until it was replenished before saying: 'Pat, you're an object of interest.'

'It's my size,' said Dawlish. 'Who's interested?'

'Mrs Black,' said Tim. 'What did you say her name was – Ethel?'

'Eileen.' Dawlish did not look round, while Black's companion approached the bar, and ordered a gin-and-Italian. She sat on one of the bar stools, lovely, but a little incongruous in an evening gown of pale blue. She half-smiled at Dawlish, but beyond a nod of recognition he made no response.

At seven-fifteen, the dinner gong went.

Dinner at the Lodge was a punctual meal, for Pierpont insisted that if the guests were not on time, they could not get the quality they would expect. So now began a slow stream of people heading for the large dining-room. Dawlish was about to join them when Woodley entered the room, and then made a bee-line for Dawlish.

'I'm glad I've found you, Captain Dawlish – I think you should know at once that we've found your uniform.' There was a marked change in his manner. 'It was in the shrubbery. The blood stains on it suggest that whoever killed Smith was wearing it. Can you spare half an hour?'

CHAPTER 5

Uniform Regained

Woodley spoke in a low-pitched voice which carried only to Dawlish's ears. The large man's expression remained unchanged.

'Yes, of course. But what about a drink first?'

'I really – '

'I won't take no,' said Dawlish firmly, raising a hand to summon the bar-man. Those people who remained looked towards Dawlish and the policeman; they included Eileen. Dawlish fancied she was smiling, and that she was amused at something concerning Dawlish's party. 'Eric, another beer – or would you prefer something short, Inspector?' He lowered his voice. 'I'd much rather the residents thought this a friendly chat, you know. Odd ideas could get about otherwise.'

Woodley smiled, a little repressively.

'Oh, all right – beer, please.' Only half-a-dozen people now remained in the bar, including Dawlish's group, Eileen, and a thickset man in evening-dress. Even at Marsham Lodge few people changed for dinner in the war days. A dinner-jacket was a rarity; full regalia was so odd that it had made the man noticeable at once. He had a reddish skin, large but not uncomely features, and gingerish hair, cut short. Dawlish guessed him to be a northcountryman.

He went at last. Eileen remained, until Black appeared in the doorway.

She turned at once, and walked with him towards the dining-room.

When the room was empty, Dawlish said:

'Here we are, then, Inspector. Can we talk?'

Woodley looked at the other two, and hesitated.

'I think – '

'My fiancee, Miss Felicity Deverall,' said Dawlish, 'and Captain Jeremy. We're all in it together, Inspector, don't try to prise us apart.'

'We-ell – '

'I hope you won't insist on the strict application of rules and regulation,' said Dawlish. He beckoned Eric, and ordered refills, to be taken to a corner table. Woodley said a little awkwardly:

'All right, Captain Dawlish – it doesn't matter a great deal where we talk, and if you like your friends to know what has happened, that's all right with me.'

'What is it all about?' asked Felicity easily.

Woodley cleared his throat.

'It concerns Captain Dawlish's missing uniform. It was found beneath some laurel bushes not far from the spot where Smith was discovered, and there was a considerable amount of blood on the right sleeve and side of the tunic. There were spots on the trousers and the shoes, also.'

'Good heavens,' said Felicity blandly.

Woodley went on:

'There are no papers of any kind in the pockets, and nothing to suggest that it's yours, Captain Dawlish, except that it appears to be your size.'

'And so it should be,' said Dawlish righteously, 'I paid enough for it.'

'There are no name tags,' Woodley assured him. 'Now, sir – do you mind telling me more fully how you lost it?'

'I wish I knew,' said Dawlish.

He made a statement of what he did know, and what inquiries he had made, and at the end of that a sergeant came in and called Woodley aside. It appeared that a servant at one of the houses on the road opposite the Lodge had seen a car draw up, driven by an officer. She knew no more than that, and she was in the room which Pierpont had put aside for the use of the police.

'Did she see him clearly?' Dawlish asked when Woodley relayed this information.

'She said he's a big man,' said the sergeant.

Dawlish said lightly: 'Well that must be fairly obvious, I think, if he was wearing my uniform. You'd like her to see me?'

'If you don't mind – we'd better get it cleared up as soon as we can,' said Woodley. He now gave the impression that he was in no way suspicious of the possibility that Dawlish knew anything about the murder, yet Dawlish fancied that the sergeant was nothing like so well-disposed towards him.

Dawlish was, in fact, beginning to feel the stirring of a real excitement.

From the time he had spoken to the gardener, and the gardener had complained about the speed with which weeds grew, he had been either on his own or with Felicity and Tim until the second sight of the porter, and the cry which had heralded the discovery of the body. No one else, with the possible exception of the dead man, had seen him.

No policeman could fail to miss the importance of that fact.

Moreover, his uniform had been 'stolen'. It was not a thing which happened often to uniforms, and in a hotel of the kind that Pierpont controlled, it was so odd that it was almost incredible. Yet Dawlish had reported it stolen.

Now, it seemed, it had been found, with the name tags missing, and bearing ample evidence that Smith had been killed by the man wearing it. No policeman worthy of the law could fail to see the way circumstances pointed towards Dawlish. A simple transition of the statements he had made, for instance, would suggest in an unbiased eye:

'*Dawlish was on his own, or with only close friends, when Smith was killed. Dawlish could have worn his uniform, killed Smith, buried the uniform under a bush, donned his slacks, and then returned to his friends and the Lodge, affecting surprise when he heard of Smith's death.*'

Much depended, of course, on the maid who had seen the car draw up.

'Is there any way in which you can definitely identify the uniform?' Woodley asked.

Dawlish said slowly: 'Ye-es. Apart from general appearance, there's a tobacco-ash burn on the left pocket, and another on the trousers – the left leg.'

'Good!' Dawlish fancied that the Inspector's heartiness was a little forced.

They passed the dining-room, where Pierpont was making his statement to the residents. Dawlish grimaced when he thought of what many of them would be thinking, in view of the policeman's interview in the American bar. Others, if not the police, would soon be looking at him with suspicion.

They reached the office, and Woodley turned to Tim and Felicity.

'You won't mind waiting for a few minutes?'

Felicity shook her head.

'Only too glad,' said Tim, and took Felicity's arm. 'Us for the bar again, Fel, I feel the need for a stiffener.' They went off, and Dawlish entered the office. Two plainclothes policemen, and a middle-aged woman dressed in maid's clothes under a rain-coat, looked at him with interest.

Woodley turned to her.

'I'm sorry to keep you, Mrs Lee, but we're very anxious to get an idea of the type of man you saw. Mr Dawlish is a big man. Was the driver about his size?'

The woman regarded Dawlish steadily and at some length. She was thin and sharp-featured; the word 'sour' came to him involuntarily. Nor did he like the way her lips tightened as her scrutiny developed. It was with absurd relief that he heard her say:

'Aye, that's the size on him. But I wouldn't know if it *was* him.'

'We weren't asking you that,' said Woodley.

'But you meant it, didn't you?' said the woman shrewdly. 'Anyway, I only see the back on him.'

'Was he fair?'

34

'He wore his hat, didn't he?'

Dawlish's relief grew apace. For a moment he had thought the maid was about to identify him – a mistake, but the kind of mistake which had been known to happen and could lead to disastrous consequences.

'All right, Mrs Lee.' Woodley was brisk, and the maid was ushered out by one of the policemen. Dawlish lit a cigarette and looked at Woodley through a haze of smoke.

'Well,' he said. 'What do you make of it?'

'It's rather early to say,' said Woodley.

'Ye-es. She isn't going to help you a lot, is she?'

'She's helped us with the size and build of the man we want to interview,' said Woodley.

'Could she describe the car?'

'I'm not quite sure.' Woodley's statement was a transparent lie, and Dawlish reflected with sombre amusement that Woodley was beginning to suspect him very strongly; Woodley, in fact, might well have suspected him from the moment of finding the uniform, but had preferred, at first, to give the opposite impression. 'Now the uniform, Mr Dawlish – '

Dawlish bent over the uniform, which was spread on a white sheet behind the desk, and began to examine it. After a moment or two he pointed to the two small burns where hot ash had fallen from his pipe.

'That's mine, all right.'

'Good. Where were the name tags?'

'At the back of the collar and the waist-band.' He inspected the two places, and saw that not only had the tags been taken away, but that the stitches which had held them in position had been carefully pulled from the cloth. At a cursory glance there was nothing to suggest that tags had ever been there. At a closer inspection the stitch-holes could be discerned.

'That's odd,' said Woodley. 'I wonder why our man took them off?' He looked at Dawlish, making a great show of frankness.

'I wouldn't know,' said Dawlish easily.

'Of course not! Now for my report, Captain Dawlish, will you confirm the statement you've already made. I shall have to find where every one in the hotel was at the time of the murder, of course. The theft of your uniform makes it clear that someone either resident or with access to the Lodge committed the crime.'

'Hardly clear,' said Dawlish. 'The man wearing the uniform might have seen the deceased after the crime, you know. However, what you really mean is that you want an account of my movements during this afternoon. Is that it?'

Woodley eyed him evenly.

'You can put it that way if you like, sir. You quite understand that – '

Dawlish smiled.

'I quite understand that at the moment I look like suspect Number One, and as such I'll help you just as much as I can.' He made a comprehensive statement, which the sergeant took down in shorthand, and then went on: 'Is there anything else?'

'Mr Smith was seen walking in the grounds shortly after Mr and Mrs Black's arrival, so that I'm particularly interested in anyone's movements after, say, five o'clock. Where were you between five and six? In the shrubbery all the time?'

'Pretty well. Before going to it I had a word with the porter.'

'Oh, yes – he's reported that.' Woodley smiled. 'I don't think there's anything else at the moment, Captain Dawlish. I'm sorry to have taken up so much of your time.'

'That's perfectly all right,' Dawlish said. He found Felicity and Tim in the bar. Felicity's expression was strained; clearly they had seen, and had been discussing, the possible implications.

'Well?' asked Tim.

'There's no definite identification; but I'm in a spot all right.'

Felicity spoke a little bitterly. 'Why did they have to take *your* uniform? Why not someone else's – there are a dozen other officers in the hotel.'

'It's a question I've been asking myself,' admitted Dawlish. 'Was it an accident – or did they take mine because they particularly wanted to embroil me in this? And if they did – why?'

CHAPTER 6

Comes The Dawn

Tim Jeremy stared at his friend in amazement, while Felicity moved restlessly. She was alarmed for Dawlish, and she knew also that whatever happened now, he would not leave the Lodge until the truth was known. Nor could she expect him to.

'*What's* that?' demanded Tim. 'No, damn it. Be reasonable, old boy. Positively no connection – it *must* have been an accident.'

'Why "must"?'

'Well, I mean, it stands to reason.'

'Don't be a jackass,' said Dawlish a little wearily. 'It doesn't "stand to reason", or anything like it. My uniform was no better fit for the wearer than two or three others here. Let's suppose that there *is* some funny business going on at the hotel – something apart from the murder, I mean. Let's suppose it's thought that I'm down here because I'm interested in Black. What better way would there be to put me out of action for a bit than to get me in cold storage on suspicion of murder?'

'No, hang it,' said Jeremy weakly.

' "Hang" is not a nice word to select in the circumstances,' said Dawlish a little moodily. 'I don't like the way things are shaping, and I don't think Woodley is quite the white-haired boy that we at first took him for. However, food.'

'You can't go into dinner like that,' said Tim, looking disapprovingly at his creased slacks.

'We'll have some sent in here.'

'And start more tongues wagging,' said Felicity.

'Well, there doesn't seem much choice,' said Dawlish. He frowned, and then smiled. 'When you really start thinking about it, there is a funny side! We've come down here to keep an eye on Black, quite sure that no one would think we were doing more than taking a few days off – and, lo! some joker selects me as the Aunt Sally. On the whole, nice work. *And* you can't say that I took the plunge into this deliberately, sweetheart.'

'Why don't you borrow a uniform?' asked Felicity.

'Where from?'

'You've just pointed out that two or three men are about your size,' said Tim. 'It's an idea.'

Dawlish nodded appreciatively. 'For the evening, yes. For dinner, no. I'm a lot too hungry, and it would mean disturbing someone half-way through. I don't feel as naked as all that,' he added, 'but I do wish I'd brought a change. However – *Eric!*'

'Waiting, sir,' said Eric from behind him.

'We're going to have dinner in here – see what you can arrange, will you?'

The meal, when it came, was quite a good one. They finished a little before the first stragglers returned to the bar, and soon afterwards Dawlish approached a tall man in uniform. It transpired that he had a spare uniform with him, and gladly placed it at Dawlish's disposal.

At nine o'clock, resplendent in borrowed plumes, Dawlish stretched his legs in front of him and regarded the others, who had just returned to his room after a tour of the hotel. It appeared that Pierpont had done no more than make a bare statement of the truth to his guests, but it also appeared that Dawlish's absence at dinner, and the way in which Woodley had approached him in the American bar, had caused considerable comment.

'It would,' said Dawlish. 'Oh, well, we'll get over it. But the more you look at the situation, the worse it seems. Even you two can't swear that I was with you the whole time. I was out of your sight for at least twenty minutes. That would be time enough to change into uniform, do the fell deed, and then change back and come here.'

'Sounds unnecessarily complicated to me, said Felicity.

'Ye-es. Only Woodley wants a murderer, and already has his eyes on me. It wouldn't be surprising if he gets busy on the telephone and tries to find whether I'm doing any under-cover work.'

'I wish we'd never come,' said Felicity despairingly.

'I wouldn't go quite so far as to say that,' said Dawlish coaxingly. 'Let's have a stroll through the grounds, and see what's happened.'

They were followed by a plainclothes man at a discreet distance, and that made the fact of Woodley's suspicion stand out clearly; nor would it be missed by the residents. They learned, again from Woodley, that a small car had been found in a group of trees a quarter of a mile away from the scene of the crime. Woodley volunteered the statement, asked no questions, and went back to his borrowed room.

Dawlish eyed Felicity grimly.

'What do they usually say at this point? The net closes, are, I believe, the right words. That's all Woodley needs for a cast-iron case. I could have gone to the car, changed, done the deed, changed back, taken the car away and returned to you, all in a matter of half-an-hour. You could both be ac-cessories after and/or before the fact, for that matter.' He was frowning despite the lightness of his tone. 'I just don't believe it was an accident. The theft of the uniform *could* have been coincidental, but to do the rest of the job so that it pointed to me is cool and deliberate scheming. It has a thoroughness that we've learned to associate with the Hun, too.'

'If there wasn't a war on, we wouldn't think of the Hun,' declared Tim.

'A sage remark,' admitted Dawlish. 'However, there *is* a war on. Has anyone any ideas?'

Neither of them had.

Woodley put in no further appearance, and Dawlish saw nothing he could usefully do, since all his movements would be suspect. Twice during the evening he saw Eileen Black looking at him; each time he imagined that she was smiling at some secret joke, and in his mind was the uneasy thought that she knew of the net which had been so carefully drawn about him. He tried to shrug the thought away, but it persisted.

By eleven, he was in bed.

It was one of those occasions when he repented his arguments against marriage. It would have been far, far better to have been able to talk to Felicity about it, rather than Tim. And on her own, Felicity would be worried and probably sleepless. It was two o'clock before he finally went to sleep.

Even then, he awakened with the dawn.

The daylight streaked unevenly across the floor as he lay looking out of the window, wondering at the sense of depression which filled his mind. It was a minute or two before he remembered what had happened. At once he struggled into a dressing-gown, and made for Felicity's door. He tapped lightly, and whispered her name. At once the bolt was drawn back, and the door flung open. She was dressed, and when he went in she put her arms about him.

'Hallo, darling!'

'Good-morning, my sweet. A rotten night had by all, I take it?'

She nodded.

Dawlish kissed her fondly. 'A pity we couldn't have enjoyed it together. As it is, I could do with a cup of tea,' he said. 'Do you think they'd be up as early as this?'

'Somebody is. I heard steps along the passage twenty minutes ago.'

He thought nothing more of it, then. 'Let's press the bell and see what happens.'

Nothing did.

'It probably wasn't a maid. I'll tell you what, I'll get some clothes on and we'll go for a stroll. Yes?'

'Yes, I'd love it!'

He was gone less than five minutes, and they went downstairs together. A clock in the hall chimed a quarter past six. The front door was open, and a policeman in the porch touched his helmet. Another watched them walking across the grounds, and Dawlish reflected that there would be more stationed round about, and that nothing he did was likely to remain unobserved.

With one accord he and Felicity turned their backs on the shrubbery, and strolled towards a meadow which belonged to the Lodge. Skirting a small herd of Guernseys, they walked towards the far side, where trees grew abundantly. The grass deadened their footsteps, as well as those of a policeman who strolled, as if casually, some hundred yards behind them.

Dawlish scowled, one eyebrow higher than the other.

'Curse and confound the flatfoots. I don't like being shadowed. What do you say to leading them a dance?'

'It might make it worse, besides, they're only doing their duty. I should think it was worse for them than for us.'

Unrepentant, Dawlish glanced about him, at the clear blue sky and the morning sun, which promised heat for the rest of the day. He drew Felicity to a thickly wooded patch with a stile and started to climb over. A thick carpet of pine needles had deadened their footsteps, so that they heard nothing until quite suddenly a voice, from ten or fifteen yards away, said clearly:

'I tell you it can't be done.'

Dawlish and Felicity stiffened, then stopped dead still. That low-pitched voice was clearly recognisable. It was Eileen Black's, and she did not sound pleased.

A man's voice, also pitched on a low key, answered her.

'It's quite time you learned that I don't accept the word "can't", my dear. This matter is urgent, and the disturbance at the Lodge must not be allowed to delay it. You have the instructions – act on them.'

'I tell you – '

'And I tell you, my dear,' said the man, and in his voice there was more than a touch of impatience. 'See that Raymond acts strictly according to instructions – he should know by now how foolish it is for him to go astray. The consequences could be disastrous – for you both.'

Dawlish and Felicity stepped quickly to one side, glad of the cover which the pine trees afforded. They heard muffled footsteps, audible only because they were heavy, and then they saw Eileen Black, walking back on the path they had just left.

In her hand was a small envelope, and she was tucking it into the neck of her dress.

Dawlish whispered:

'Try to keep her in sight. I'll take the other customer.'

Felicity nodded, and slipped away, while Dawlish ducked beneath the lower branches. He heard a slight movement ahead of him, but it was some time before he caught a glimpse of the man who had given such definite orders to Eileen.

A large man.

A man, in fact, about Dawlish's height and build. He was walking with long, easy strides, a brown-clad figure, very much the type one would expect to see in the woods on a morning in early September. He carried a walking stick, and once or twice swept at a branch.

He appeared to have no idea that he was being followed.

Dawlish went after him very silently, and then he saw the end of the wooded patch, and beyond, another meadow. It would not be easy to conceal himself there, and he had to choose between risking being seen, and losing his man. He had not made up his mind when he heard a movement to his right, and then he forgot everything but the threat which was offered with devastating suddenness.

For a second, smaller man had suddenly appeared. He was holding a small automatic, and it was pointing at Dawlish.

CHAPTER 7

Near Thing

The man, no higher than Dawlish's shoulder, had thin, sharp features, now puckered up as if he were tensing himself for the act of shooting.

Dawlish jumped backwards, then dived for the trees.

He heard a slight sound, no more than that made by a stifled sneeze, and then something cut its way through the branches. He could just see the legs of his man, while he looked about him quickly for a small branch which could be turned into some kind of weapon.

A second 'sneeze' and more rustling.

'He's not very near,' Dawlish muttered to himself, 'but he's near enough. I wonder where the other johnny is?'

He saw a fallen tree-branch, and picked it up.

He felt less frightened than angry, although he was scared enough to be cautious. The trees were all young, and none gave him complete cover. Dawlish crept low, but he was seen, for a third 'sneeze' came.

A bullet buried itself in a tree not two feet from him.

There was a chance that the sharpshooter would have only half-a-dozen bullets; on the other hand he might have plenty of ammunition, and since there was so little sound from his gun, he could feel safe from interference unless Dawlish shouted to attract attention.

This, Dawlish did not want to.

There were things about this little sharpshooter that he badly wanted to know, and he did not think he would learn much if either of them fell into the hands of the police just then. Afterwards he admitted that his decision had at least a degree of folly in it, but he did not think twice at the time.

Above him the trees were thicker. He stretched to a fairly stout branch and hauled himself from the ground.

A fourth shot rang out.

Dawlish drew his legs up with alacrity. The bough only just bore his weight, but it enabled him to reach a higher one. He could now see the top of the little man's head; and he saw something else.

The big man had joined the hunt.

He too had a gun. Dawlish kept quite still. Five minutes passed. The men began moving around, and Dawlish could hear them clearly.

'Did you see him?'

'Yeh.'

'What was it?'

'That fella. Dawlish.'

'You're sure?' The big man's voice strengthened with those two words.

'I got eyes.'

'Could he see me?'

' 'Ow the 'ell should *I* know?'

The big man muttered an imprecation. Dawlish waited until they were well ahead of him, and then climbed down. The path of pine needles made silent following a simple matter, but he kept at a safe distance. It was, however, too far to hear what was said.

By the second meadow, he stopped.

The trees gave him shelter, but not his quarry. They walked across the meadow, apparently not perturbed by the possibility of being spotted by the police. Dawlish could see the big man in profile.

It was a strong face, and not unhandsome. Next to him, the sharpshooter looked a little shrimp of a fellow, taking two steps to the other's one and barely reaching his shoulder.

There was a stile further along the hedge which divided the meadow from the road; they climbed over it, then disappeared. Dawlish played with the idea of running across the meadow and following them further, but decided against it. Instead, he chose a longer route, going through the trees, climbing over a wire fence, and then walking along the grass path bordering the road on the other side. When he drew within sight of the stile he saw that the little man was standing behind the hedge, with one hand in his pocket.

Dawlish smiled.

The walk across the meadow was now fully explained. The men had realised the possibility that he would follow them, and the little one was now waiting, with gun handy, to put paid to his efforts. Dawlish hesitated, knowing that he would be running a considerable risk if he revealed himself, when he heard footsteps on the road.

They were slow and deliberate; the tread, he imagined, of one of the policemen.

The little man looked quickly along the road, and then glanced over the meadow. Satisfied that the latter was empty, he climbed the stile and disappeared. Dawlish walked at speed along the road, but when he turned a corner he saw only an empty stretch of some half-a-mile ahead of him.

The man in brown might have gone either way.

Dawlish turned, and then saw that his guess had been right; a policeman was approaching him, staring at him fixedly. Dawlish smiled pleasantly.

'Good-morning, constable.'

' 'Morning, sir.' The man hesitated, seemed about to put a question, and then changed his mind. 'Nice morning, sir.'

'Yes, isn't it. Any luck at all?'

'Depends what you call luck,' said the constable cryptically. Dawlish hid a smile, and then went back along the road.

At the second meadow, where the cows were grazing, he climbed the wire fence. From the wooded patch two policemen emerged. They had followed him and Felicity, of course, and had been searching for them amongst the trees.

Dawlish saw no more men in uniform, but in the grounds of Marsham Lodge Frederick was busy with his interminable fight against weeds. He said so, strongly. Apparently he was either unaware of, or unaffected by, the general feeling that Dawlish was in some way connected with the murder.

Two or three early-morning residents nodded distantly.

Dawlish went on to the Lodge, and reached his room as Felicity came from hers. Tim, still in his dressing-gown, wandered in from the bathroom. He wanted to know, with some indignation, why the others hadn't called him.

'When one means to walk warily, three's a crowd,' said Dawlish succinctly. He turned to Felicity.

'Did anyone else see you?'

'Only the policemen.'

'Did Eileen know you were following her.'

'I don't think so. I let her get across the meadow before I followed. She went in at the side door without turning back.'

'Hmm,' said Dawlish, leaning back in an easy chair. 'It must have been Eileen you heard going out so early. What about some tea?'

'I've just ordered it.'

'Splendid!'

Jeremy, standing squarely in front of the window, said witheringly:

'And now if you *don't* mind, what's it all about?'

Dawlish explained, shortly and to the point. That finished, he drank another cup of tea and lit a cigarette. No one spoke, until Tim rubbed his hands together with macabre glee.

'Well, we're in it now, friends!'

'Don't gloat,' said Felicity. 'And you've got to rejoin your regiment today, anyhow.'

'Tomorrow,' declared Tim. 'I was going to spend a night in London, but while this is on, I stay here!'

'Hark to the optimist!' Dawlish blew smoke towards the open window, and watched it swirl out as it was caught by a slight breeze. 'If I keep out of jail for the rest of the day that'll be as much as I've a right to expect. I'm quite sure Woodley will want to know all about the morning excursion. And *I* want to know all about the trigger-happy strangers. However, if I'm to be down at a reasonable hour, I must shave.

Keep an eye on the Blacks, one of you, and if they're both down at breakfast, let me know.'

Felicity looked at him helplessly.

'I suppose you're going to look for that envelope?'

'You can bet your lovely face that I'm going to look for it,' Dawlish assured her. 'And it won't be my fault if I don't find it. On the whole,' he added as he began to run hot water into the basin, 'we've reached an interesting point. Large man in brown, powerful personality, probably a resident locally. Little man, clearly a hired thug, but one who isn't scared of his employer, or he wouldn't indulge in back-chat. Mysterious instructions. Eileen protests that it can't be done, large man says it can. Presumably Eileen has instructions for Raymond as well as herself, and Raymond Black isn't the kind of chap to take kindly to instructions unless – '

He paused.

'Go on,' said Tim. 'Don't drag it out for effect.'

'It wouldn't occur to you that one has to think sometimes,' said Dawlish with dignity. 'Unless he's taking them, orders I mean, from a higher official. A German one,' he added grimly.

Tim went off in search of the Blacks, and in fifteen minutes returned to say they were both downstairs.

'When do we start?' he demanded.

'Actually you should stay outside and keep an eye open for maids,' said Dawlish thoughtfully. 'There are two rooms. If we're looking in the bedroom and someone starts to open the door, we can slip through to the drawing-room in time. The two of us will make a quicker job of it. What time do they get the beds made, do you remember?'

'Not too early, they're short of staff.' Tim opened the door a couple of inches, and then closed it, turning sharply. 'I say, Pat, do you think the big cove you saw was the Smith-killer?'

'Dawlish stared at him.

'Do I *think?* By Saint Peter, do you want it handed to you

48

in three-letter words? Of course I think so – I very nearly know so. What do you use for a mind?'

'No, hang it – '

Dawlish gripped his arm with rough affection.

'Tim, I wouldn't have you one whit different. You're an everlasting source of enjoyment, and the only reason your mind doesn't work at speed is that you don't use it enough. Have a try now – we want to run through those rooms in something under fifteen minutes. Suitcases and clothes first, I think.'

'Right!' It did not occur to either of them to hesitate, for they wanted the envelope which Eileen had been given, and they wanted also anything else which might prove incriminating or informative about the Blacks.

No one passed them in the passage.

'If I hadn't brought up their baggage I wouldn't know the rooms,' said Dawlish. 'Here we are.' He tried the handle, and the door opened easily. He grimaced. 'They'd probably have locked the door if they'd left much that was worth seeing,' he added. 'I don't think this is going to yield results, my son.'

'Well, get inside and start,' urged Tim.

They stepped into the sitting-room. The communicating door was open, and there was also another sight that interested them. A settee was untidy with blankets and a pillow, suggesting that someone had slept on it the previous night.

'Very, very chaste,' murmured Dawlish. 'There's nothing else here.' He stepped to the communicating door, and widened it. The bed was tumbled and untidy. Suitcases, lying open, were on the floor. Three drawers of the dressing-table were also open, but none of those things made Dawlish stop short.

What did was a reflection in the dressing-table mirror.

He could see the wardrobe, and the little space between it and one corner. Squeezed into the space was the red-faced, squarely-built man, who on the previous night had made himself conspicuous by wearing evening-dress.

CHAPTER 8

Chunky Man

Dawlish gave no sign to Tim that he had seen anything amiss, but stepped towards the dressing-table and then turned sharply to the wardrobe.

'Come out of there!'

Tim, opening his lips to protest, looked in the direction of Dawlish's gaze.

The expression on the face of the man standing there was a peculiar mixture of chagrin and alarm.

'What are you doing here?' he asked.

'And *you?*' demanded Dawlish politely.

'If you aren't aware that you are already in a somewhat invidious position, I must point it out to you,' said the man. He had a mellow and surprisingly attractive voice, and in his eyes there was a twinkle which Dawlish did not miss. 'Supposing you take your hands away from your guns, gentlemen, and behave a little less like actors in a melodrama?'

Dawlish smiled. 'Well, as we appear to be two to one, perhaps you will give us an explanation of yourself first.'

'I can see that this might be a little difficult, and as you will realise we can't stay indefinitely in a bedroom to which we have no right, perhaps we can go to one of the others? Mine, or yours – whichever you prefer.'

Dawlish's eyes swept round the room.

'You appear to be a pretty cool customer. Where haven't you looked?'

'In the wardrobe.'

'I suppose I must postpone asking you what you were looking for,' said Dawlish, stepping to the wardrobe and opening it. 'Keep the gentleman well under cover, Tim, while I run through this stuff.'

It took him five minutes.

Apart from the rustle of clothes, the occasional chink of a hanger on metal rods and a squeak when he opened one of the three small drawers, there was no sound. He found nothing – no papers, no money – no gleanings from any pocket.

He turned back, and closed the door.

'Our Black is evidently a cautious man,' he said. 'That's a pity – I suppose you didn't find anything?' As he spoke he went to the suitcases, picked one up and began to examine it for a false bottom. The strange man said drily:

'I've tried that – there's nothing the matter with them.'

'Ah-h.'

'Don't play the fool, and don't waste time, Dawlish,' the other said urgently. 'We're crazy to stay here – and neither one nor the other can do anything about it. If I report finding you in here, there'll be questions asked. If you report finding me, the questions will prove even keener – unless I misjudge Woodley.'

Dawlish shrugged.

'That about sums it up,' he agreed, 'except that I can ask questions of you and stand a much better chance of getting answers than the other way round. The two-to-one odds, you see. All right, we'll get along to my room – '

'Wouldn't it be wiser to go downstairs?' demanded the other. 'We'll be missed if we're much later. We could have breakfast at the same table, and continue our talk afterwards.'

Dawlish raised an eyebrow.

'Nicely worked out. But – '

'Don't make the situation untenable, Dawlish,' the man urged. 'If you can satisfy me that you had a *bona fide* reason for coming here, I will exchange mine for yours.' He had all the confidence in the world, Dawlsh thought: and he thought also that he rather liked the man.

It was this that decided him to act on the other's suggestion.

They reached the passage unobserved. Dawlish closed the door quietly behind him, and they walked to the head of the stairs. There he said:

'What name are you going under here?'

'Prior,' said the man promptly.

'Were you christened "Prior"?' inquired Dawlish. The other smiled, an attractive smile which strengthened Dawlish's liking, although it made him no less wary.

'We won't go into that. I suppose you realise that the Blacks will know the rooms have been searched.'

'I do. It ought to be interesting to hear whether they report it,' said Dawlish.

'That is precisely what I thought. We have a lot in common I think. However, we can discuss it after breakfast.' Prior led the way across the dining-room, and reached Felicity. Dawlish introduced them gravely.

During the meal Prior talked easily and well. He had a store of war anecdotes, all well-told, although in less capable hands they might have been boring. He looked about him while he talked, and both men saw the Blacks leave the room.

Prior smiled and leaned forward.

'Now for it! Raymond Black will either come shouting down to Pierpont, or he'll discreetly forget to mention it. What's the betting, Dawlish?'

'Evens,' said Dawlish promptly.

Prior intrigued him, and moreover gave the impression that he could, if he desired, give a good reason for his visit to the Blacks' rooms. Dawlish wondered whether he would be wise to tell him the truth. He was still wondering when they reached his room.

The police had shown no special interest in him, but he imagined that as soon as Woodley arrived he would be questioned again. But the depression following the police suspicions of the evening before had lifted, and he was beginning to feel exhilarated. So many questions wanted answering, so many things could happen.

He closed the door, and leaned against it.

'Well, Prior. Three to one now – Miss Deverall isn't a nonentity, believe me. Supposing you talk first?'

Prior smiled; his matter-of-factness was one of the most attractive things about him.

'I see nothing against it. But I'll be frank to start with, Dawlish. If *you* don't give me a satisfactory explanation you'll be in Queer Street.'

'Not for the first time,' said Dawlish.

'No.' Prior was clearly amused. 'So I have gathered – you have earned quite a reputation, haven't you? But on this occasion, you can't rely on that to see you through. I know quite well that you have no official reason for being here – for the simple but effective reason that *I* have. You might care to see my Special Branch authority.'

As he spoke he slipped a wallet from his pocket, and extracted a card. He handed it to Dawlish.

*

Dawlish examined the card with care.

He was less surprised that Tim and Felicity, for he had not been indifferent to Prior's calm assumption of authority.

Now he noted the signature of the Home Secretary, and also that of Sir Archibald Morely, who was his cousin. Morely was the Assistant-Commissioner at Scotland Yard, and his was a signature which could not easily be forged; Dawlish was reasonably sure that it was genuine. He handed the card back.

'You consider this to be sufficient evidence?' Prior inquired rather drily.

Dawlish nodded.

'It stands. Does Woodley know who you are?'

'He does not!'

'Nor Black, presumably.'

'I hope not,' said Prior quietly. He sat down on the edge of a bed, and looked with deliberation at Dawlish. 'Now I think it will be a good idea if you talk – and talk frankly, please. I'll say in advance that I've no doubt your motives are all they should be, but this is an affair in which we can't risk mistakes.'

Dawlish grinned.

'Go on, complete it. By blundering amateurs.'

'You won't find me over-endowed with professional jealousy,' Prior assured him, and then waited. Dawlish did not take long to prepare his thoughts, and he made a full and comprehensive statement, including the part which Crummy Wise had played in his interest in Raymond Black. Prior did not interrupt. Once or twice he frowned, particularly when Mr Smith was mentioned, while a description of the man in brown, and the fact that he had given orders to Eileen Black, seemed to interest him.

Dawlish finished at last.

'Well, I can't give you anything else, except embroidery, I'm afraid. You won't want that.'

'No-o,' said Prior thoughtfully. He was silent for some seconds while the others regarded him in varying ways, and then he said more briskly: 'No, I certainly don't want fal-de-lals, Dawlish, and you've given me plenty of good, strong material. I suppose you feel you've a rightful interest in the show?'

'While I'm being Aunt Sallied as a murderer, decidedly.'

'Well, I don't see any reason why you shouldn't lend us a hand. Heaven knows we want it!' He spoke rather bitterly, but the mood changed quickly. 'I'll have to get permission, of course, and that will take some hours. Meanwhile, you can do me a service. If Black reports, and there's an inquiry, will you keep my part quiet for the time being? I particularly don't want him to get wind of me. He's done enough damage already,' added Prior slowly. 'Two of us came down here to watch him, and only I am left. Smith was working with me,' he added, and he sat back as if prepared to study the reaction of the others to that bald statement.

CHAPTER 9

Concerning Colonel Cole

Before any of the others spoke, Prior said:

'Putting it like that sounds pretty grim, I admit. But Black must be watched by someone he doesn't suspect for a time, and he's already got his eye on you, I fancy.'

Dawlish nodded. Felicity looked at him, and there was a faint smile in her eyes. Silently Dawlish blessed her. Aloud:

'All right, Prior, I'll do that, conditional upon you sending word through to London promptly, and getting me co-opted. How much can you tell me now?'

'I don't propose to tell you anything,' said Prior. 'When things are in order I can let you know what I know. It's precious little. I – oh, there's one thing that it won't do any harm to tell you: your friend Wise was quite right. Black is a German, and he's believed to be operating on this side. We don't know who works with him, and above all we don't know how he gets messages out of the country. We want to find out, and we want to get his whole mob – that's why we're holding our hands where Black himself is concerned. This man in brown is the most likely, at the moment, but there may be others beyond him.'

'Too true there might,' said Dawlish. 'All right, we'll work on that basis. I suppose I'll be fired at from all quarters until you get word from London – Woodley on the one side, Black on the other.'

'You can take it,' smiled Prior.

'It looks as if he's got to,' said Felicity a little coldly.

Prior turned to her. 'I'm sorry, Miss Deverall, but war is no respector of persons. Now I wonder if one of you will look into the passage – I'll slip out on my own, I think, I don't want to be associated too much with you.'

'Well, having breakfast together was your idea,' said Dawlish drily.

'A meal's one thing. Gathering in rooms is another.' Silently Prior slipped out, leaving the others to regard each other with varied expressions.

Dawlish began to hum under his breath.

'And so we're in it, and the first thing is to find what Woodley proposes.'

Woodley proposed nothing.

He arrived about eleven o'clock, and asked why Dawlish had been out so early that morning. Dawlish answered that he had gone out for a stroll. He was puzzled by Woodley's attitude, for the policeman was clearly bent on worrying him as little as possible; possibly the 'reputation' was a big factor in that.

At half-past eleven, Dawlish and Felicity left the Lodge. There had been no report from Pierpont or the servants about a burglary in Black's room, and that suggested that Black was not going to make a complaint. It also suggested that he might try to handle Dawlish personally.

'I wonder how long it will last?' Felicity said. They were in Dawlish's Lagonda, and going along the drive of the Lodge. 'I suppose Prior is all right?'

'I propose telephoning from Ringwood,' said Dawlish. 'He'll tell me if the chap's a fake. One way and the other we seem to be pretty firmly enmeshed in this business, my sweet. However, there's no reason to start expecting bullets to spring out of hedges or cars to block the road. You're not nervous, are you?'

'I have felt safer,' admitted Felicity. 'I can't forget the savage way Smith was attacked.'

'I'm bigger than Smith,' said Dawlish stoutly.

There was only one thing of interest to them on the run to Ringwood, some ten miles from the Lodge. A car with a fair-haired woman driver followed them. It might have been coincidental, but neither of them thought so. The driver made no attempt to hide the fact that she was following them, but nor did she allow herself to get near enough to be recognised.

'It could be Eileen,' said Dawlish as he pulled up into the car park near the market place of the little country town. 'On the other hand, fair hair is no-one's copyright. She's dodged along on the by-pass, and is coming in the other way, I suppose. Will you keep your eyes open along the High Street?'

Felicity did so, knowing that Tim Jeremy was watching Raymond Black, and believing that no positive danger could threaten while Tim was doing that. She pushed thought of the man in brown to the back of her mind, as well as of the little man who had been with him, and who had fired what Dawlish presumed to be a powerful air-pistol, for he knew of no silencer which could have so effectively silenced an automatic.

From a kiosk in a side street Dawlish telephoned Scotland Yard, and after some difficulty spoke to Sir Archibald Morely. One thing was settled almost immediately.

'Oh, it's you,' said Morely, a little disparagingly. He did not consider it wise or necessary to encourage Pat Dawlish by show of admiration or enthusiasm; for that matter Morely rarely enthused about anything to anyone. 'What are you up to now?'

'Who have you heard from?' asked Dawlish.

'The Winchester police, and Prior.'

Dawlish said sharply: 'So Prior's all right?'

'He's perfectly all right,' said Morely. 'I'm seeing the Home Secretary in an hour's time, and I expect he'll give you a *visa* for the job. Be careful, Pat, and look after Felicity.'

'I'll do both,' Dawlish assured him. 'Prior will be able to tell me the whole show when the O.K. comes through, I take it?'

'I don't see why not,' admitted Morely.

'Good man. And thanks,' said Dawlish. He rang off, and then walked along the High Street. Felicity was looking in a shop window, and did not look round until he stood beside her. Then she said quietly:

'It was Eileen.'

'Nice work. Where is she?'

'She's gone into a shop on the other side of the road – for coffee, presumably.'

'Hm-hm. Still watch her, darling – and reassure yourself about Prior. Morely's given him a clean bill, and half-promised me one. How are you feeling about it?'

Her eyes were smiling, those wide-set, grey-green eyes he loved so much.

'Better.'

'That's fine, said Dawlish. 'Now I'm going to look for my man in brown. It's pretty crazy, I suppose, but we might get a line on him fairly soon. And as we're in it, we may as well work with what speed nature endowed us.' He chatted for a few minutes, and then walked back towards his car.

It *was* pretty crazy; the chances of a meeting with the man in brown were so slim that they hardly existed, yet there were some things which made Dawlish feel that the man lived in, or near, Ringwood. It was unlikely that he would have walked with such a disregard for being seen had he not been sure that whoever saw him would not be surprised. Only a local resident, surely, and one who lived fairly near the Lodge, could safely feel like that at half-past six in the morning.

Of course, Woodley would probably know the man from his description. But so far Woodley was to know nothing of the deeper issue.

Dawlish found himself brooding over the events of the past forty-eight hours. Crummy's round and amiable face was often in his mind's eye. Crummy would give a lot to be down here. Crummy –

Dawlish stopped reflecting.

He was passing a newspaper shop. There were no posters outside, and only one paper left in the rack hanging from a nail in the fascia board. The paper was the *Mid-Hants Gazette*, which meant no more to Dawlish than if it had been the *Timbuctoo Times;* what did matter was the photograph on the front page – a full-face photograph of the man in brown.

He caught the headline, which read:

Colonel Cole Addresses Local Farmers.
Need For Greater Effort.

'Well, well, well,' said Dawlish, and he went inside and bought the paper. He was thinking, as he came out, of his astonishing luck. He had the man's name, his address – virtually everything he could have reasonably hoped to find that day – in a matter of minutes; and he had bought the last paper; had he been ten minutes later it might well have disappeared from the rack.

He read the article as he went along.

Colonel Cole, it seemed, had delivered a strong and stirring appeal to local farmers, urging a greater war-effort. The opening words of the article told Dawlish much:

'Colonel Graham Cole, of Ley Manor, prominent agriculturalist and one of the foremost war-workers in the county, addressed a crowded meeting of local farmers and farm-workers in the New Hall, Ringwood, on Friday evening. Colonel Cole said – '

'Admirable sentiments, Colonel,' murmured Dawlish as he read a line or two, and then folded the paper. 'Ley Manor, now I wonder how far that is from the Lodge?' He nipped into the Post Office, and consulted a directory. In it was a map, showing the bigger farms and houses within a fifteen mile radius of Ringwood.

Ley Manor and Marsham Lodge were in adjoining estates.

'And so we get better and better,' soliloquised Dawlish. 'I wonder if Eileen has come in to see the gentleman, or whether she just followed us because we're annoying her? I think an hour or two alone with Eileen might help things along.'

He doubled back to where he had left Felicity; but

Felicity was not there. He walked the length of the High Street again, but did not see her. Then he looked for Eileen Black's car, which had been parked in a side street.

The car was gone.

Nor was Eileen in the cafe which Felicity had seen her enter. Dawlish retraced his steps hurriedly, half-expecting to find Felicity waiting in the Lagonda.

The car was there; Felicity was not.

Frowning, puzzled, and for the first time a little worried, Dawlish began to walk along the High Street again, but he did not get far. A soldier in battle-dress – one of quite a number – stopped him.

'Pardon me, sir – are you Mr Dawlish?'

'That's right,' said Dawlish.

'Gentleman asked me to give you this, sir.' The man passed over a folded slip of paper. 'He couldn't stop as he was in a hurry. Good-morning, sir.'

Dawlish opened the note, breathing quickly, and a little afraid.

His fears were justified. He read:

> 'Come and see me, if you want to see Miss Deverall. Ask for Ley Farm Cottage, and don't talk.'

Just that. No hysterical or melodramatic threats; a calm enough order, inferring far more than it said. 'Ley Farm Cottage' made it easy to associate the note with Colonel Cole, and Dawlish wished he had asked the soldier more about the man who had given it to him. He had been so concerned in that moment for Felicity that he had lost the opportunity. It was completely gone, for the man might be one of the dozens within sight, or even have left the town.

Dawlish brushed a hand distractedly over his forehead. He still wore the borrowed uniform, but he had telegraphed to a London friend to send on one from his flat. He hesitated, and then climbed into the Lagonda, planning to ask at the Post Office for Ley Farm Cottage. He did not start the engine immediately, however, for a car drew alongside, and

60

in it was Eileen Black. Her face was tense and drawn, and her voice just loud enough for him to hear:

'Don't start your car. Don't start your car.'

Then she drove off, and he sat staring at the back of the Austin as it disappeared towards a bridge at the far end of the town.

CHAPTER 10

Odd Fact

Dawlish frowned, and shifted in his seat, one hand on the gear lever, and a foot on the clutch. The fierce intensity of the woman's expression, the low-pitched urgency of her voice, had not faded with her going.

'*Don't start your car – don't start your car.*'

Dawlish sat holding the wheel, deep in thought; then he opened the door and climbed out. He was anxious for Felicity – not a desperate anxiety but a deep, nagging worry, for the words of the note had impressed him. That anxiety conflicted with Eileen Black's warning.

He reached the front of the car and threw up the bonnet-lid.

Until then he had been frowning, but now the muscles of his face smoothed out and he became quite expressionless. He saw the small container, no bigger than a match-box, resting on the cylinder-head. It was attached by a thin piece of wire to the self-starter. The wire was at a tension, and when the self-starter was pulled the match-box would be jerked away.

Very gently, he lifted the container.

Without closing the bonnet, he carried the box along the narrow street towards the river bridge. There were several people about, but none on the river or its banks. He resisted a temptation to examine the contents, and tossed it over the bridge, so that it fell in the water twenty or thirty feet away from him.

He *saw* the explosion.

The moment of impact brought it about, and he saw the

water divide and then rise upwards, saw an ever-widening circle moving towards the banks on both sides, as well as the smoke and the flame, although the flame was soon extinguished. There was nothing left of the box, even when the swelling, writhing waters had subsided, and the smoke had cleared.

He was aware of pounding footsteps. By the time he turned, he saw at least a dozen soldiers in battle dress hurrying towards him. He knew that he was in a spot from which it would not be easy to escape. Not far away a policeman advanced steadily, while a small crowd of passers-by were openly staring at him, aware only of the explosion and the possibility that he had some part in it.

The deafening effect of the noise faded.

The ring of soldiers broke when a lieutenant appeared, and then Dawlish had one of the breaks which, he felt, were overdue. It was a man he had seen at Marsham Lodge; his wife was staying there while he himself was billeted in Ringwood. He and Dawlish had chatted for twenty minutes on the previous afternoon.

He gave Dawlish a quizzical look.

'*Now* what are you up to? Haven't you caused enough sensation for a day or two?'

'I've a nasty feeling that I haven't really started,' said Dawlish. 'The sensations have been made for me – '

'A victim of circumstances, I know,' said Lockwood drily. 'I suppose you want me to pacify the police?' He turned as the policeman came up, and his voice sharpened. 'It's all right, Constable, some fool dropped a hand-grenade, and this gentleman tossed it into the river before it did any harm.'

The constable looked from one to the other. 'I'm afraid I'll have to have particulars, sir.'

Half a dozen questions followed which Dawlish was compelled to answer.

He gave his name and his temporary address. The whole business took about a quarter of an hour. At the close of it, Lockwood, a fair-haired youngster who had made it clear on the previous day that he knew of Dawlish's reputation, slid a hand into his pocket, and said:

'Well, what really happened?'

'A joker put the explosive inside the bonnet of my bus. Actually it was a damned ingenious idea,' added Dawlish. 'A pull at the self-starter, and off would go the balloon – or that's how it should have worked.'

Lockwood's smile disappeared.

'Good God! But how did you –'

Dawlish put a hand on his arm.

'A tip off. And as soon as I can, I'll pass it on, but things are difficult at the moment.'

Lockwood took the hint.

'Good man,' said Dawlish, and then he wondered whether Lockwood could help him, for someone must surely have seen Felicity go away. Lockwood could ask questions without taking it any further, for at the moment Dawlish did not want the police to know anything about her disappearance. It would be worth half-an-hour's delay to get some information, and he put it to Lockwood immediately.

Lockwood nodded at once.

'They're all due at the hall for a lecture in ten minutes, and I'll put it to them before it starts.' He frowned. 'It's going to be a bit ticklish – what kind of story ought I to pitch?'

Dawlish thought for a moment.

'Let's see, what about this? Felicity's lost a ring; did anyone notice it being picked up by a stranger? That'll get them talking. Of course they might not remember her –'

Lockwood chuckled.

'Don't be an idiot! There won't be one who didn't notice her – she's pretty well as noticeable as you – though in a very different way!' He went off at once, while Dawlish watched the stream of men in battle dress converging on a hall not far from the cinema in the High Street. He wondered anxiously whether it was wise to delay, and then decided that it was.

Nevertheless, he would have to go to Ley Farm Cottage, as soon as he had worked it out, even though the note and the

64

invitation held all the qualities of a baited trap. He did not like traps. Certainly he did not like the idea of visiting the cottage on his own. There was not a great chance that he would find Felicity there, for it was at least possible that she had been taken somewhere else. Nor was there much doubt that they – he thought actually of Black and Cole as 'they' – would gladly see him dead. If his visit to the cottage worked as they had planned, the probability was that he would not come out alive.

His mind returned to the same question.

Why had Eileen warned him?

It could be that she disliked the work on which she was engaged, or disliked it taken to the point of murder. But he was not satisfied by this explanation, any more than he was satisfied with the thought of going unattended to Ley Farm Cottage. That 'they' would expect him to rush after Felicity was certain; but he needed time to consider, to make sure what was the best course; a direct approach was certainly ill-advised. It was unlikely that they would harm Felicity because he was some time in carrying out the instructions.

In short, if they wanted to kill her they would lose no time. Dead or alive, she would be a bait for Dawlish.

Dead or alive.

The thought frightened him, and he fought against it, telling himself that it was absurd to think that they would kill her. Why *should* they kill her?

But he was not comforted, knowing by now, that the men were utterly ruthless.

They would think that Dawlish would pass on some of his discoveries, and he believed that they were trying to stop this, at all costs to himself. In view of his reputation, which sprang immediately to Lockwood's mind, and to Woodley's for that matter, they would not think that he had started on the affair by little more than chance. They would assume that he had authority, and they would act accordingly.

Half-an-hour passed, miserably.

Then Lockwood came out of the hall. Dawlish hurried across the road to meet him.

'Well?'

'Get on the pavement,' said Lockwood tersely. 'Look out!' He jumped to one side, and Dawlish followed him.

It happened as quickly as that.

A car zoomed past them with a roar and a gust of wind that sent them both off their balance. Dawlish was swung about, for the wing of the car actually caught at his coat. Thus he saw the driver, a little man with a ferrety face, and with his lips drawn back over thin, pointed teeth.

He might not have noticed those details but for the fact that he had seen the man before.

He was Colonel Cole's morning companion.

Lockwood reached the pavement first, a little shaken.

'By George, that was a near one! Didn't you see it coming?'

'I did not,' admitted Dawlish. 'I wasn't in a mood to look much about me – sorry, Lockwood. You're all right?'

'Oh, yes – and you?'

'I think I've a tear in a borrowed uniform,' said Dawlish grimly. 'Did you have any luck?'

Lockwood grinned.

'They'd noticed her all right! They haven't seen a ring, but they did see her walking into a cafe with another woman.'

'Did they notice the other woman?'

'An oldish one, I gathered. She didn't make the same impact as Miss Deverall! The cafe's down the other end of the High Street – *Betty's Cake Shop*.'

'And they actually saw her go in?'

'Oh, yes. I say, Dawlish, what the devil is the matter? By the look of you anyone would think she'd been kidnapped!'

Dawlish said: 'Yes, wouldn't they? And they might even be right.' He gave Lockwood no chance to make any comment, and while the expression on the lieutenant's face was changing from inquiry to amazement, he added: 'Are all your fellows at the lecture?'

'No. There's a company free – they came off duty this morning.'

'Can they visit *Betty's Cake Shop* pronto? Everything on me,' he added quickly, 'and they can buy the shop for all I care. I'm not joking, Lockwood, this is serious. She didn't go of her own free will. The cake shop should tell me something, but it mightn't be wise for me to be there alone.'

Lockwood stared: 'Good – Gad! Yes, all right, I'll send 'em along. I wish to heaven I could come myself, but I'm late for a lecture already.' He hurried off, an earnest and worried young man, while Dawlish forced himself to walk slowly towards the end of the High Street. Before he had reached the cafe, five or six privates and two N.C.O's had passed him. He let them go in first, and then he followed.

A grey-haired woman bustled in from a room behind the shop.

'Good-morning, boys! You're in earlier than usual this morning – what is it you want?' She took orders for tea and coffee, and then looked at Dawlish.

'And for you, sir?'

Dawlish smiled.

'I'm looking for a young lady who came in here half-an-hour or so ago with an older lady – do you know where I can find her?'

'Two ladies?' The grey-haired woman frowned in concentration. 'I don't think they came here, sir. I've been on duty all the morning – what were they like?'

Dawlish described Felicity, but the woman's face remained blank, and she repeated:

'I don't think they came here – in fact I know they didn't. I don't forget customers, sir, not even occasional ones. You must have made some mistake.'

CHAPTER II

'Some Mistake?'

For the moment Dawlish was non-plussed.

The woman's statement was made so calmly that it was almost impossible to disbelieve her. He wondered whether Lockwood's men had made a mistake – it was certainly possible, although Lockwood had seemed sure enough of his men's powers of observation. Dawlish had been prepared to be told that Felicity had been and gone, but not for a downright denial that she had ever been there.

The point-blank statement made it difficult to know what to do, but his indecision was broken by the cockney voice of one of the men.

'Nar then, Missus, you must'a forgotten. She come in alright – I see 'er. You don't forget a face, nar, do yer?'

The woman snapped:

'I don't, and she didn't come here!'

'I ses she did,' said the Cockney decisively.

The woman shrugged and turned towards Dawlish. Her expression was strained, and she was gripping her hands tightly together. 'You've made a mistake, sir, I'm sorry I can't help you. Do you want anything?'

Dawlish said:

'Yes, the lady.'

'I tell you – ' the woman backed slowly away from him, then turned and bolted into the back room. Startled faces turned towards Dawlish, and several of the men rose to their feet. Dawlish said quickly:

'Will some of you get round the back, and make it snappy? There's an odd show here, and I think we'll find my friend –

if we hurry.' As he finished speaking he vaulted the counter. When he reached the door, four of the soldiers had gone out into the street, and the others crowded behind him.

The door was locked.

It was a flimsy thing, and he put his shoulder to it, finding that it gave way with little trouble. He stumbled forward as it opened, and so he did not see the two men and the woman at the top of a flight of stairs.

A door leading to a kitchen and thence the garden was open. Dawlish hesitated, wondering if the woman had gone that way, and then one of the men called:

'She's gone upstairs.'

He turned, and saw the woman of the shop at the head of the stairs. In her arms was a heavy chair, and as he looked upwards, she let it go.

It thudded down step by step until it hit the floor, one leg breaking off. Behind him a man swore, another said:

'The hellcat! Would you believe it?'

A smaller chair followed the first.

The staircase was very narrow, barely wide enough for a man of Dawlish's size to walk without brushing against the sides, and there was no chance of dodging anything that was tossed down.

He called out:

'Watch all the windows, will you?' and then started up the stairs as the woman, and a man whom he saw behind her, carried a small chest of drawers and placed it across the top step.

It completely blocked the way, and Dawlish was forced to crouch beneath it. A man's voice came to him from the other side:

'Dawlish, if you don't clear the shop we'll cut her ruddy throat.'

So Felicity *was* there.

The statement sent relief through Dawlish, absurd though that might seem. Felicity was here, not at Ley Farm Cottage, and he was within a few yards of her. It made him take a chance that he would not otherwise have done. He stood up, tested the wedged chest, and began to clamber over it. The man lashed at him with a small poker, but the blow glanced off, doing little damage.

The woman of the shop had a china bedroom jug in her hands, and she raised it high before crashing it down, aiming for his head. She missed, for he shot out a hand deflecting her aim. The jug broke into a hundred pieces, scoring marks across the top of the chest.

Dawlish hauled himself over.

The man had gone into a room on the right, but had no time to close the door. Heavy footsteps on the stairs told him that more of Lockwood's men were in his wake.

He entered the room.

He saw Felicity, although he recognised her only from her clothes, for a towel had been swathed about her head and face. Two men were near the window, waiting, as a forage cap slowly appeared. In the hand of one of the men was a knife.

Suddenly he turned, and lunged with it towards Felicity.

There was no time for Dawlish to reach him, and most movable objects had been sent down the stairs. Dawlish did the only thing that was possible. He stooped, put both hands beneath the brass-railed bedstead. Felicity was between it and the far wall. The man drew within a yard of her, and then the bed tipped up, and knocked against him. He staggered and as he did so the forage cap developed into the Cockney soldier, who leapt from the window. In seconds he had wrenched the knife away.

Dawlish left the men and the woman to the soldiers, and reached Felicity's side. The towel in which she was swathed seemed endless. He could not find the end, or the beginning, and it seemed ages before he had finally uncoiled it.

Dishevelled, scarlet in the face, Felicity stood, taking in great breaths of air, as he supported her.

She was trying to say something to him, and for a moment Dawlish stared at her in alarm, seeing for the first time that there was froth on her lips. *Froth – foam –*

And then he realised what she had been trying to say.

70

'S-s-s-soap in m-m-my mouth,' gasped Felicity. 'Ugh!'
Not until he had located the bathroom and she had been able
to rinse her mouth with a dozen glasses of cold water did she
feel better. That they had pushed a cake of soap into her
mouth to prove an effective gag, and followed up with the
towel to make sure she could not get rid of it, was obvious.
Dawlish did not need to ask many questions, and he did not
feel like asking them. He was too relieved.

*

The presence of the soldiers made anything in the nature
of a private interrogation of the three prisoners impossible,
and the obvious thing for Dawlish to do was to get in touch
quickly with the police. He did not have to wait long, for
the constable who had already seen him at the bridge
entered the shop as Dawlish arrived downstairs.

The policeman gazed at Dawlish, with a somewhat grim
expression.

'*Now* what have you been doing'?'

'Constable, there isn't time for a full explanation,' said
Dawlish. 'This young lady was abducted by the people in
the shop – the people are upstairs – and I found her here. I
want you to tell Chief Inspector Woodley of that immediately, and to give him my name – Dawlish, do you remember?'

'*I* remember all right. But Mr Woodley's from Winchester
– '

'He's handling the case,' snapped Dawlish. 'The murder
of a man near Marsham Lodge.'

To do the policeman justice, he wasted no more time.
While he was telephoning the local station, a corporal had
taken it on himself to make coffee and he brought in a cup
for Felicity and another for Dawlish. They were drinking it
when the policeman returned from the telephone.

'As it happened, sir, Mr Woodley was at the station – he's
coming right over.'

'Good,' said Dawlish. 'Have a look at the trio upstairs,
will you? Some of them might be strangers.'

Two of them were.

The men were not known in Ringwood, and the regular staff of the cake shop, it transpired, had been sent out earlier that morning, leaving only the grey-haired woman in charge. What there was to learn from her Dawlish did not know. He did know that Woodley's attitude towards him had changed. He was, he said, very glad that nothing worse had happened, and he hoped Miss Deverall would not feel the effects of her rough treatment too much. The three prisoners would be taken immediately to the police-station, and they would be interrogated there 'as soon as instructions were received'.

Dawlish did not ask from whom the instructions were likely to come. He gathered that Woodley had been told by the Home Office that Dawlish was working on special orders, and he also gathered that Woodley felt he should have been told so on the previous evening. The prisoners were not likely to be of great importance, Dawlish thought, and it transpired that he was right.

They refused to make any statement, refused also to identify the woman who had taken Felicity to the tea-shop. As far as Dawlish and the police were concerned, they were no further ahead. His own puzzle concerned Eileen Black.

Why *had* she saved his life? For he was not fool enough to believe that had the explosion occurred while he had been sitting in the car he would have escaped.

He was back at Marsham Lodge by the middle of the afternoon. He had seen Prior, who confirmed that he had had the necessary instructions from London; Prior was to increase Dawlish's knowledge of the case within the next half-hour. He had not yet told Prior, or anyone else, of his recognition of Colonel Cole; the time for that would be when Prior made his statement.

There was at least some cause for satisfaction.

The tea-shop, clearly a meeting place for the lesser members of the Black-Cole organisation, was closed for good, and he could congratulate himself that he had not hurried immediately to Ley Farm Cottage.

'We'll visit it,' he said slowly as he looked at Felicity. 'Feel like telling Tim and I how you got lured into the cafe?'

'Oh, Pat, and I thought I was being so clever!'

Dawlish raised one eyebrow above the other, and Tim leaned forward in expectation. '*Now* we're about to hear things.'

Felicity laughed, a little on the defensive.

'Well, she *did* look rather a dear old thing – the woman, I mean – but when she came up and asked me whether she hadn't seen me before, I didn't really think it was genuine. So I let her talk, and then she suggested a cup of coffee. I didn't see any harm in that – all the tea-shops have windows from which you can see the street – and Betty's looked a charming little place. But as we went inside a man clapped his hand over my mouth, and someone closed the door. I just didn't have time to think, Pat, and when I did start thinking it wasn't very good. What an idiot I was!'

'When did you last see her?' Dawlish asked.

'At the shop, of course.'

'As you went in, you mean.'

'No, upstairs – in the bedroom.'

'*What?*' Dawlish's expression hardened.

'Just before you arrived,' insisted Felicity. 'I heard your voices downstairs, and I tried to shout – that's why they used the soap. I – Pat, she's one of the prisoners, isn't she? I took that for granted.'

Dawlish said slowly: 'Well, well, well! The nice old lady disappeared, but she certainly didn't go out of a window or a door.'

CHAPTER 12

Nice Old Lady

The 'nice old lady' who had so nearly succeeded in creating a diversion which, for Dawlish, would have been a tragedy, slipped along an alley-way between the cafe and the next door premises, and, bending low, hurried to the end of the garden and then to a field which was close to the main street of the town.

In it was a barn, once left derelict but now used for storing emergency bedding in case of air-raids. The old lady stepped into the barn, tightened her coat about her, and from a shelf took a mackintosh which reached almost to her ankles.

It served her purpose.

Wearing it, she walked across a footpath to the far end of the town, and then mixed with a crowd which was waiting for a bus. She kept looking along the High Street but tried to hide her nervousness. Once or twice she started as men appeared to come straight for her, but they passed. A policeman was standing thoughtfully on one side of the road. The bus was overdue, and the crowd grew impatient; the old lady's cheeks grew pale with the suspense, but at last a green double-decker came in sight. There was room for all of them, and the old lady climbed to the top deck.

'Ferndown, please,' she said to the girl conductor.

Even the ting! of the girl's bell-punch made her jump, and she stared out of the back window several times, lest she was followed. No private car tailed the bus, however, and she grew more settled in her mind.

She alighted at Ferndown and entered a telephone kiosk near one of the newly built shops.

She gave a Ringwood number.

There was a long, suspenseful wait before a sharp voice answered the call.

'Who is that speaking? I'm in a hurry.'

'It – it's Mona,' said the old lady in a voice which shook a little. 'I – I'm at Ferndown, I thought – '

'What's happened?' The voice grew urgent.

'I can't explain on the telephone,' she said. 'Can you send a car for me?'

'Yes,' the man said abruptly, and rang down.

She waited for nearly three-quarters of an hour before a car drew up near her. She climbed in, glancing behind her, as if to assure herself that she was not being followed.

The car drove steadily on to a large house not far from Marsham Lodge. Once there, the woman alighted and hurried into the house. No one saw her as she went up the stairs to a room which she called her own. She was shaking a little as she took off her mackintosh and tidied her hair. That done, she went along a passage and tapped on a door.

There was menace in the voice which bade her come in.

Entering, she saw a man sitting behind a large desk. Dawlish would have recognised him at once from the photograph in the local paper. He ignored the woman for fully three minutes, then barked out:

'What happened?'

The woman's voice rose to a whine.

'I – I did all I could,' she said protestingly, 'it wasn't my fault. I couldn't help it!'

'You can never help anything that goes wrong,' he sneered, 'but if it goes right it's always thanks to you. Well, out with it.'

She told the story with many hesitations and pauses, and while he listened his strong and powerful face grew bleak. She finished at last, staring at him as if afraid that he would strike her.

'Dawlish didn't give us a chance, I've never seen any one move like it!'

'I'm getting very curious about that man,' the other said

75

slowly. 'Very curious indeed. Do you know what else happened? He was either warned of the little present put in his car, or he suspected something like it would happen. It's strange, my dear.' He was looking at her again, and the note of menace was back in his voice. 'It's very strange, isn't it?'

'Y-yes, but I don't know how – '

He stood up so suddenly that she jumped, and then backed away from him as he rounded the desk and approached her. As he gripped her shoulders with cruel force, every vestige of colour went from her cheeks.

'Don't, don't!' She found her voice at last. 'You're hurting me.'

He said in an even voice.

'Are you sure you know nothing about it? You didn't tell him?'

'No, no! I wouldn't do such a thing, I've never even thought of it!'

The man released her, pushing her away impatiently.

'I hope you're telling the truth,' he said. 'If you're not – ' he paused again, lost in thought.

He said at last: 'Someone told him. He can't have guessed it.'

The woman nodded eagerly, afraid to risk speech.

'Someone gave us away. We'll have to find out who it was, and when I get him – '

'Him?' repeated the nice old lady. 'Him, dear? Are you sure it's a man? It might be a woman, you know.'

'What do you mean?' he snapped.

'You know what I mean.' She broke into a little giggle. 'Don't tell me you've fallen at your time of life for a pretty face, dear.'

He shouted at her, obscurely, hideously. 'Out! Out!'

Safe at the door she paused cunningly. 'There's something about that girl I wouldn't trust, my dear.'

'Get out!' he yelled.

The door opened and shut.

The man stayed sitting at his desk unmoving. His expression remained hard and calculating; but there was now a hint of uncertainty in it.

He said aloud:

'Can she have told Dawlish?' He paused. 'And who *is* Dawlish, just what part is he playing? I can't believe he suspects anything, no one can – yet.'

Finally he shrugged his shoulders and picked up a newspaper lying on his desk. It carried his own photograph. He read the words beneath it, smiled derisively, then pulled a pad towards him, and began to write notes for a similar speech to the one which had earned so much publicity.

It was an hour before he had finished.

He had forgotten Dawlish while he had been writing, but now memory came flooding back. Again he asked the questions he had already put to himself, but was no nearer an answer. He was worried. There was something about the man Dawlish that disconcerted him. The fact that he had deliberately lifted out the charge in his car, and thrown it into the river, showed a presence of mind and an ability to get ruthlessly down to main issues.

Could the girl have passed on the information?

It was possible, and he would have to find out. The only thing he was sure of was that he could not trust Mona.

*

The police had searched the premises of Betty's thoroughly, but found no trace of a woman answering the description Felicity was able to give. Dawlish had lost his satisfaction with himself; he should have questioned Felicity earlier, and yet it had not occurred to him as feasible that anyone who had been in the tea-shop when he had arrived could have escaped.

An old man busy in the garden next door had been an interested spectator of the whole affair. No one had left the shop by the back door that morning he averred – he was quite sure of it. Nothing shook him from his statement, and because of that the police made an even more thorough search of the shop. But it was Dawlish – who realised that in

77

the bedroom where the melee had taken place the wall-paper was applied in panels – an expensive decoration, for so small a place. A test of the walls showed what he had half-expected; there was a hidden door, operated quite simply by pushing against it.

It showed a small room, leading to a narrow alley between the shop and the adjoining premises. Through that alley the 'nice old lady' had doubtlessly gone.

Nothing else was found.

With these facts firmly established, Dawlish returned to Marsham Lodge. There Prior was waiting; and there Dawlish told of Colonel Cole, of Eileen's warning and of the near-accident when the ferrety-faced man had nearly run him down. All of those things Prior digested carefully, and then:

'I suppose you're quite sure of Cole?'

'I could be more sure if I saw a profile photograph,' said Dawlish, 'but there isn't much doubt.'

'I'll get hold of one – Woodley will find it for us. He has some idea of what we're doing.'

Dawlish pursed his lips. 'What do you know about Cole?'

'He's one of the more influential landowners about here – a power in local politics, and strongly tipped as the next Member of Parliament. He's not a farmer, but he owns several local farms, and subsidises them himself. I looked him up, as well as the other local gentry, but they all seemed quite impossible to visualise as villains in the piece. However, Cole gave that note to Eileen Black, and he's been after your blood. That proves our case as far as we're concerned, though we'll have to get a lot more evidence before we can do much.'

'Why?' demanded Timothy.

Prior smiled, but not with humour. He looked pale and harassed, and was not so self-possessed as when they had first met him.

'We wouldn't need it for a straightforward police case, of course, but for our show we want everything. No half-measures this time.' He pressed a hand against his forehead.

'I've had instructions to tell you what I know Dawlish, but it doesn't cover Miss Deverall or Captain Jeremy.'

Tim stood up with a grin.

'That means we're both *de trop*, Fel.' He held out his hand.

'Thanks,' said Prior, but he still seemed distrait, even when the door had closed on the others. 'Well, now, where had we got to?'

'You admitted that Crummy Wise was right about Black.'

'Oh, yes.' Prior looked far from well. There were dark patches beneath his eyes that had not been there the day before. He took a tablet from a small bottle, swallowed it, and replaced the cork slowly. 'When I do get a thick head these aspirins don't seem to touch it.'

'Aspirins?' Dawlish spoke sharply.

'Yes, why?'

'Aspirins usually have a screw-cap, not a cork, for a stopper.'

'This did have – I lost the cap,' said Prior. 'Don't get an idea that anyone's poisoning me, I take pretty good care! But I'm rather at sixes-and-sevens. I'm a little sorry about the showdown in Ringwood, as a matter of fact.'

Dawlish stared, saying nothing.

'That sounds a bit ungrateful, I know,' said Prior. 'But obviously it was a rendezvous, and now it's closed up it will make our local gentry more careful. In fact they might move.'

'If Cole's concerned, he can't very well.'

'No, I suppose not. Well, it's no use beating about the bush any longer. Here it is. There's an organisation in the south of England, whose business it is to get farming facts.'

Dawlish said: 'Can't you be more concise?'

'I wish I could, but you'll just have to get the picture as I go along I'm afraid. There's a big agricultural effort on as you know. Cole's leading it down here, that's one of the things that's worrying me. As far as I understand the show, the Nazis have cooled off invasion for the time being, and are putting everything into the blockade. Well, they can't stop us growing what food we can in England – *or can they?*'

Dawlish frowned.

'I don't quite get you.'

'Well, supposing they did find a way of putting grit in the farming industry? Supposing they held up a lot of the new crops? That's the possibility. I haven't been told all about it, but I do know that Whitehall's worried because there are rumours of trouble on the farms. For one thing there's been an unusual lot of foot-and-mouth disease. A big area in Dorset is affected, and another in Wiltshire –'

Prior broke off.

'*Blast* my head! Give me a drink, will you – water will do. That aspirin stuck in my throat.' He coughed again, while Dawlish fetched a glass with water. He disliked the pallor which had spread to Prior's cheeks, and the darker patches under his eyes – patches which seemed blacker now than they had been ten minutes before. Earlier, Prior had looked seedy; now he looked a sick man.

Yet on the previous day he had been in glowing health.

'Thanks.' Prior took a mouthful of water, swallowed, and then choked. The glass dropped from his hand. He stared at Dawlish, his eyes widening, and for the first time he showed signs of alarm.

'The – the damned stuff wouldn't go down!'

Dawlish said: 'Is your throat sore?'

'There's a lump in it.' Prior coughed again. When at last he could speak he gasped: 'Dawlish, for God's sake help me!' His chest was heaving then, as if he could hardly breathe, and Dawlish stepped to him, lifted him from his chair effortlessly, and carried him to the window. The fresher air seemed to do him good, and his breathing grew easier.

Dawlish pressed the service bell.

For once it was answered promptly, and May appeared.

'Oh, May – there is a resident doctor, isn't there?'

'Yes, sir. Dr Millsham.'

'Ask him to come up at once.'

'Yes, sir.'

Prior forced himself to speak as the door closed.

'That – that wasn't nec – ' he broke off again. There was something terrible in the sight of him, trying so desperately to breathe, and in Dawlish's feeling of utter uselessness.

A tap on the door heralded Dr Millsham.

As might have been expected at the Lodge, the resident doctor possessed an easy, confident manner. He appeared to be the type of man in whom patients would have full reliance, one capable of maintaining the health of the residents while pandering to their minor ailments. Dawlish saw him frown as he set eyes on Prior.

'Hallo, what's this?' He waited for no answer. 'How long?' he asked sharply.

'No more than ten minutes,' said Dawlish.

'No previous sore throat, or – ' Millsham stopped, obviously quickly immersed in his diagnosis. When he had finished, leaving Prior gasping for breath, he said: 'Help him on to the bed, will you?' He opened his case, took out a hypodermic syringe, and a small bottle of iodine. He handed the latter and a wad of cotton wool to Dawlish. 'Clean a spot in his neck, just in front of the ear, please.'

Dawlish obeyed, like a man in a dream.

Prior lay motionless except for his stertorous breathing, and he made no movement when Dawlish took off his collar and tie, and then rubbed the iodine over a small patch of skin. Millsham filled his needle, and then took Dawlish's place. Prior's breathing grew heavier, and more laboured. His body heaved once or twice, and his face was contorted.

Millsham said in a low voice:

'It might work. Five minutes will tell us. Take his other arm, will you, he might get violent.'

The warning was all too necessary.

As Prior's breathing grew yet more laboured his body heaved, and it took all of Dawlish's strength and Millsham's to keep him on the bed. Perspiration poured from him, his mouth worked, his nostrils were distended. Millsham exerted considerable pressure on his arm and shoulder, and watched steadily.

Seconds ticked by.

Each second seemed a minute, and a minute seemed an age-long period. Dawlish glanced from time to time at his wrist-watch, but the hand seemed motionless. But it *did* move.

Two minutes.

Three.

Four.

The patient's convulsions subsided gradually, and to Dawlish it seemed as if he was breathing more easily, though each breath caused an agonising rasp, and the veins in his neck stood out like cords.

At the end of the fifth minute, Dawlish spoke:

'Well?'

'I think we dare move him – he'll be in hospital for a month or more, but he's lucky to be alive. Watch him, will you?' Millsham said nothing more then, but went out, and Dawlish heard his footsteps fading. In the room the silence was broken only by a shrill whistling in Prior's throat, a mad medley of discord.

But it grew quieter.

Dawlish looked away from the bed for a moment, and his glance fell on the door. He stared, for beneath it a piece of paper was being pushed, slowly at first until suddenly it skidded across the polished floor and stopped against the edge of the carpet.

Dawlish saw his own name on it, printed in big block capitals.

CHAPTER 13

Curt Message

There was no time, that was the trouble.

There was no reasonable breathing space between one thing and the next.

Dawlish had been concentrating on Prior's sudden seizure, and what it might imply. While watching the man he had been thinking of the headaches of which the other had complained, of the curious fact that he took aspirins out of a corked bottle – the explanation was ample, of course, yet the fact remained odd – and of the speed with which the seizure had developed. He had pondered on Millsham's prompt and capable handling of the emergency, and he had been wishing the man would return, when he had seen the envelope.

Dawlish stretched forward, and getting the envelope between his fingers, drew it towards him. He had fought against a temptation to see who had pushed it under the door; only Prior's plight, the fact that he must not be left, had stopped him. Dawlish studied the envelope. Anyone might have printed his name. There was nothing else on it – just: '*Captain Dawlish*'.

He was about to open it when Millsham returned, bringing two middle-aged women, one dressed in a nurse's uniform, with him.

'Any change at all?'

'None.'

'Good.' Millsham bent over the unconscious man. 'His breathing's easier. I think he'll pull through. There's an A.R.P. ambulance on the premises, and we can use that to get him away – Winchester Hospital will be best, I think. I'll telephone them.' Millsham was very crisp and businesslike. 'Are you going out immediately?'

'No. And I'd like a word with you as soon as you're through.'

Millsham nodded. 'Of course. I think it will be best if this is kept quiet. The hotel has been sufficiently disturbed already.'

'I shan't talk,' said Dawlish a little sharply.

'Of course not!' Millsham gave instructions to the nurses, and Prior was taken from the room. Millsham went out, leaving Dawlish alone.

He allowed his shoulders to slump for a moment under a nagging weight of depression. He could not believe that Prior's seizure was an accident, and he associated it with the aspirins. He had taken the bottle from Prior's pocket, and it was now in his own.

He slit the envelope and withdrew a slip of paper. On it was printed:

'First, Smith. Second, Prior
Third – why not Dawlish? Why
don't you go away, Captain?'

Dawlish raised an eyebrow. He did not doubt that it had been composed by the writer of the message which had concerned Felicity.

First, Smith. Second, Prior.

Prior had been so anxious to make sure that he was not discovered and identified, yet his efforts had been useless. Clearly, this note was calculated to shake Dawlish's nerve, just as the first message had been. The timing in both cases was perfect.

Prior had not even been able to tell his story. The effect of the poison – it must surely have been a poison of some sort – had made it impossible for him to marshal his thoughts. Had that been judged to the moment, also? Had the people who had delivered the message realised that Prior would not be able to talk?

Probably not, thought Dawlish; they could only put the stuff into the tablets, they could not be sure when Prior would take one. That, of course, presumed that the seizure had been brought on by the tablet the man had taken so shortly before. Was there any reason for thinking otherwise?

Dawlish said aloud:

'Of course there isn't! I wonder – '

He was about to ask himself whether Millsham could be wholly trusted.

There was a tap on the door, and Millsham came in. His expression was grave and anxious, but he was talkative enough. The effect was of an irritant poison operating on the throat, he said, causing swelling of sufficient dimensions to cause suffocation. The injection, which had eased the swelling, had taken temporary effect, but there was no real certainty that the effect of the poison would stop at the throat. A diagnosis had been impossible, and it might take some time for one to be made.

Dawlish revealed the aspirin-bottle. He had already examined it, finding that the label bore the name of a well-known manufacturing chemist. He told Millsham what little he felt the man should know, and was surprised when Millsham said:

'I think this will help us, Captain Dawlish. I understand, of course, that you're not in a position to be wholly frank.'

Dawlish eyed him evenly.

'Why, doctor?'

Millsham shrugged.

'I hardly think you need telling, Captain Dawlish. The least said the better, of course. But I do hope the Lodge will soon be free of intrigue, it gives one a most uncomfortable feeling!' Now that the emergency was past, Millsham was becoming the portentous doctor of fashion Dawlish had expected from the first. 'You will report the matter to the police, of course.'

'Certainly. But I'd like you to make a report at the same time,' said Dawlish. 'And I'll keep a few of those tablets, I think.' He extracted three, then handed the bottle to Millsham.

The doctor went off smartly, while Dawlish, moving to the window, contemplated the grounds. Frederick was weeding; while a few of the residents were sitting about in deck-chairs. A peaceful lull seemed to lay over the garden.

After ten minutes, Felicity and Tim returned.

They had no idea of what had happened, and a startled silence followed Dawlish's explanation. Then almost in the same breath they spoke.

'Then this means – ' began Tim.

'You'll replace Prior,' Felicity said tensely.

'It could be,' admitted Dawlish. 'But truth to tell I don't feel too happy about working with anyone else. I haven't been told the whole story, and I can't be sure that something isn't happening behind my back. Prior kept his tale until the last minute, and it proved too late. Something to do with farming, I gathered, and foot-and-mouth disease – ' he broke off, and shrugged. 'A big subject, and it's too early to start guessing. But there are some things we can do.' His face brightened. 'Yes, we can get down to Eileen and Black, for instance. There's no one here to hand out instructions, so why wait for them?'

'What's the idea?' asked Tim.

Dawlish smiled.

'We do to Eileen what a little old lady did to Felicity. I think Eileen might talk, since she's already shown that she's well-disposed towards us. Do you feel like acting the beautiful siren, darling?'

'On whom?' asked Felicity.

'Eileen, of course,' said Dawlish severely. 'If there's anything to be done about Raymond, I'll handle that gentleman myself.' He smiled at her. 'If I thought that Black was susceptible I *might* let you work on him, but he looks too cold a customer to be shaken by beauty. I wonder,' he added slowly, 'why a bed was made up on the settee in their rooms?'

'You mean they might only be pretending to be married?' demanded Tim. 'What's the sense in that?'

'Well, obviously they'd have a better chance to compare notes, and avoid suspicion that way. I wish I could find out what orders Eileen had from Cole this morning.'

'I suppose you're quite sure it was *Cole?*' asked Felicity.

'I don't think there's much doubt of *that*,' said Dawlish. 'Cole is our man all right. Anyhow, let's stop talking, or we won't be able to see the wood for the trees. Try to find Eileen, my sweet – and Tim will concentrate on getting Black. Once they're separated, Tim can keep Black occupied for an hour. That will give us the time we need to talk to Eileen.'

Tim scowled.

'And how the deuce am I going to hold Black?'

Dawlish smiled. 'He knows you're a friend of mine. Work on that angle. Even show hostility, if you must – it won't surprise him. But let's get the gentleman first.'

Events ran well for them.

Dawlish, walking with Tim towards the shrubbery, came upon the Blacks not fifty yards away.

It was peaceful and quiet in the garden, and death seemed a long way off.

Felicity had taken a deck-chair near the steps of the Lodge, and as they passed she waylaid Eileen with a pretty air of invitation. Black himself bowed frigidly, and went ahead.

'Good work,' murmured Dawlish. 'Your game, Tim. Keep Black in his room, and don't spare the strong arm if it's necessary. We haven't shown our hand at all yet, and it's as well that Black knows we don't like him any more than he likes us.'

Tim was already moving.

'Wish me luck,' he said.

'Earn it,' smiled Dawlish.

He appeared to saunter in Tim's wake, but actually he moved very quickly, reaching the steps as Felicity stood up from her chair. Eileen was saying:

'I do wish I could stay for a chat, but – '

'We're just going in,' smiled Dawlish, and he lined himself on one side of her. Felicity was on the other, and all three of them went up the wide staircase together. No one was in sight, as Dawlish murmured:

'I owe you a big debt of thanks, Mrs Black.'

'For what?' asked Eileen blandly.

'That's one of the things I want to clarify,' smiled Dawlish, as they reached the head of the stairs. He slid a hand to her arm, gripped it firmly, and still smiling, said:

'Supposing we work it out in my room? And don't protest or do anything foolish. We had to take the gloves off one day, you know.'

CHAPTER 14

Eileen

He felt the muscles of her forearm go stiff; then they relaxed a little, and without further protest she walked with him. He did not release her until they were inside his room. Then he closed the door, locked it, and put the key in his pocket. Felicity moved to the window.

The other woman looked from one to the other.

'What *is* this?'

'A lesson in abduction,' said Dawlish pleasantly. 'But we're not proposing to be violent; not yet, at all events. In the first place, I'm too grateful, but I'd like to know how you learned that there was an infernal machine in my car?'

She stared at him, her face showing astonishment, even bewilderment. Her acting was perfect; although it gave to Dawlish a sense of irritation, for it was that much more to overcome.

'What on earth are you talking about?'

'The kindly word at the market place.'

'What market place? I – Miss Deverall, do you know what he's talking about?'

Dawlish's eyebrow rose.

'Are we getting anywhere by this kind by argument? If it is necessary to recapitulate, you warned me not to start my car. I investigated, and discovered that had I started it, I would have been blown to smithereens. Well?'

'I think you're mad,' said Eileen Black.

Dawlish shrugged.

He noted that she was breathing a little heavily, and her breast was moving agitatedly against the white silk blouse that she wore beneath a gaily patterned coat.

89

'Do you mind letting me go?' She spoke sharply.

'Very much,' said Dawlish. 'We'll shelve the Ringwood incident, and go back a few hours. You were up at dawn this morning. You slipped out of the Lodge before it was fully light, and so avoided the police. You went across the meadow and in a thicket of trees you met a man about my size, wearing a brown tweed suit.'

He watched her closely as he spoke.

He saw the affected bewilderment fade from her eyes. It was replaced by a look of acute alarm; there was no doubt of that. Her quick breathing reminded him of Prior, and he did not like it.

'I – I don't understand you.'

'I think you will,' said Dawlish. 'He gave you instructions which you disliked. He also gave you an envelope which you tucked into the neck of your dress as you went away.'

Her lips were parted a little, and she looked towards the window, as if for some means of escape. But Felicity was standing there.

'This – this is absurd!'

Dawlish said calmly: 'I saw you. I don't believe in mirages. In any case you were followed back to the Lodge, and to your room. Where's the letter he gave you?'

She said nothing; for the first time she attempted no denial.

'The letter,' he repeated.

Then she spoke. 'All right, I *did* warn you today, I knew what was planned and I didn't want you killed. I hate all violence, I think – ' she paused, and then plunged on: 'I think its damnable that a man should be killed, so – so lightly. That's the trouble, they don't think of people. But you mustn't stay *here*, Captain Dawlish! You've been lucky to escape so far, but you won't escape the next time!'

Dawlish shook his head. 'It might be true, but it might also be another way of trying to get rid of me,' he said. 'I'm prepared to admit that I'm probably proving a nuisance to your friends, and particularly to Black. But nuisances, like lovely ladies, are born and not made. You could talk from now until Christmas and not get me away from here until my curiosity has been satisfied. Does that make the position clearer?'

'Oh, you fool!' She turned to Felicity, with her hands outstretched, as if in appeal. 'Can't *you* make him see sense? Can't you persuade him to go? Haven't you had enough trouble and danger as it is? You won't be able to do anything, even if you stay – they're too ruthless, they'll stop at nothing to get what they want. I – ' she drew a sharp, quivering breath. 'Oh, what's the use? How can I expect you to take any notice of me? But – I did save you this morning, surely that will convince you that I mean what I say!'

Dawlish said slowly:

'It could do, but I'm not sure yet. Why did you warn me?'

'I've told you – I didn't want you to die.'

'You didn't worry about Smith, or Prior.'

'Who?'

Dawlish said: 'Smith, or Prior.'

'I don't know who you're talking about. I do know that they intend to kill you. If you don't go away *quickly*, you'll – '

'I'll be a corpse by morning. I know,' said Dawlish. 'I've heard similar prophesies before, but I'm still alive, you see, and I hope to go on that way for a long time to come.'

'You don't know what you're fighting.'

'I have an idea,' Dawlish said pleasantly. 'By the way, Smith was the man killed in the shrubbery yesterday evening. Colonel Cole killed him. Prior was the man who searched your room last night. Raymond Black, presumably, poisoned him.'

'*You know of the Colonel?*'

He hardly heard her words, her hushed astonishment was so great.

He said airily: 'Yes, quite well. The man in brown.'

She raised a hand to her breast, despairingly.

'What – what else do you know?'

'More than you think likely. And I hope to know more yet, when you've finished talking, Miss – '

'You know my name,' she said quickly.

Dawlish smiled.

'Do I? I know that it isn't Mrs Black. But that isn't as important as the letter Cole gave you this morning. That, and the instructions he gave with it, instructions which you couldn't carry out, or at least didn't want to.'

She stared at him, saying nothing.

Dawlish's voice hardened.

'We can't go on like this, you know. I can turn you over to the local police, and they'll be only too glad to detain you. I can have Cole detained, and Black – most of the bunch, if it comes to that. But I'd rather know what orders you had, to start with.'

She ran her tongue along her lips.

'I – I can't tell you. You're imagining things. I'm his wife, we've been married a week. I don't know anything about the murders, Raymond doesn't, either. Colonel Cole – Colonel Cole has been blackmailing Raymond, and me – oh, God, I can't stand it any longer, it's getting worse every day, every hour, every minute! We've had to do just what he told us, he's threatened to hand Raymond to the authorities, he's made our lives a positive hell!'

She was shaking from head to foot when she finished. Felicity moved from the window, and led her to a chair.

Except for the violent shudders which ran through the girl, there was no sound in the room. Dawlish regarded her, trying to decide whether she was really so upset, or whether she was acting.

But could anyone act as cleverly and as thoroughly as she appeared to be doing? It looked to him like a nervous breakdown, a temporary collapse after a long period of strain. And her words bore that out; the blackmail statement was at least plausible. He had no reason at all for thinking that Black himself had taken any active part in the murders; he had merely assumed it.

And she *had* warned him.

She quietened after five minutes, and sipped a little of the water he had brought her.

Felicity said quietly:

'Go out for ten minutes, Pat.'

He nodded. 'All right, I'll be in your room when you want me.'

He knew that he could rely on Felicity to look after the girl – but *was* she married to Black? Or was that also part of an act?

He walked along to Black's room, and listened outside the door. He heard nothing, and then he tapped. There was no answer. He turned the handle, finding the door opened easily. The suite was deserted.

Frowning, he returned along the passage, and when in Felicity's room he rang for a maid. May appeared, and he ordered tea. As if on an afterthought he asked her if she had seen Black or Jeremy. She had – they had been in Mr Black's room together, then left it, and gone out into the grounds.

That Tim and Black should go out together was surprising, but Dawlish did not doubt Tim's ability to look after himself. It did suggest a degree of cooperation from Black which was certainly not to be expected.

When the tea arrived Dawlish carried the tray to Felicity's room and rather diffidently tapped on the door. Surely she and Eileen had finished their heart to heart by now?

He waited a moment, and then the door was opened by Felicity.

'All right, you can come in.' She murmured hurriedly: 'It's a strange story, Pat – but don't let her think you disbelieve it, will you?'

'I'll do my best to behave,' said Dawlish solemnly, and carrying the tea tray he followed her back into the room.

CHAPTER 15

Strange Story

Eileen Black's eyes showed plainly enough that she had been crying. Her hair was dishevelled, and she poked at it ineffectually – brushing one wisp back and releasing two others – as Felicity poured tea.

Sitting there she looked little more than a child.

Felicity said gently:

'Shall I talk, Eileen, or will you?'

The girl looked nervously at Dawlish, but his large, lounging figure seemed to give her confidence. She began to talk quickly in a pleasant, easily listened to, voice, and he remembered with a start that she was an actress.

'It all began two years ago,' said Eileen. 'That was when I first met Raymond. We – we fell in love at first sight – I suppose you won't believe *that*.'

Dawlish thought of Raymond Black, and found it hard to believe, until he recalled that she had been young, and Black possessed the rather showy good looks that so often appealed to an unsophisticated girl.

Not wishing to break the thread of what he hoped she was about to tell him, Dawlish merely smiled sympathetically, and after a short pause, she went on.

'I met Raymond two years ago, just after the war had started. You remember the first sirens in London, and how everyone hurried to cover? Well, I ran all right, and I started talking to Raymond in a shelter – then afterwards it turned out we were both going to the Gala – the theatre, you know. I had a small part, and Raymond had designed some of the costumes.

'Well, we saw quite a bit of each other, and I think if it hadn't been for – for his father, we would have been engaged almost at once.'

'His *father*,' said Dawlish weakly. Raymond Black was not a man who might be expected to be under paternal influence.

'Ye-es. That's the beastly part about it all. And it's this you'll find so hard to believe. Raymond, well, his name isn't really Black, it's Bache. He's German – or rather, his father is. His mother was English. He was brought up in this country, and he speaks English as well as any of us. He *is* English at heart, everyone who knows him knows that. But his father was interned on the outbreak of war, and Raymond has been afraid all the time that the same thing would happen to him. That was why he wouldn't get married – at first, that is,' she added hastily. 'But as the months went by and he was left alone, we began to feel happier. He had given his real name to the police, of course, and he registered and did everything he should do, but apparently the fact that he had only spent a few years in Germany counted.'

She paused, and Dawlish said gravely: 'I see.'

'His father was sent over to Canada,' Eileen went on, 'and then he was released, but he's still over there.'

'Yes,' said Dawlish.

'Well, that's all about Raymond and me,' said Eileen. 'We were wonderfully happy most of the time, but there was always this fear at the back of his mind. Then – then when something *did* happen. You see, when Raymond had been in Germany, three years ago, he had joined the Nazi party. Of course, he didn't realise at first what it really meant, and when he *did* he hurried back to England. I think it scared him.' She paused, then added more slowly: 'Well, someone over here learned that he had been a member. They started blackmailing him, making him pay a few pounds at a time, to keep silent. Then – then they told him to take a message from London to a village in Hampshire. All he had to do was hand the message over to a man staying at an inn. After that there were several jobs of the same kind. It – it wasn't long before we both realised that he was working for a gang of thieves. Raymond tried to back out of it, but what could he do? It was that, or losing his freedom. We talked it over, and decided to go on; we often travelled together, you see.

'Then – then there was an accident at one of the places. A man was killed.' She had lowered her voice and was speaking very quickly. 'Raymond and I knew nothing about it until afterwards, but – but Cole, yes Colonel Cole! – made it clear that we could be charged with the murder. Somehow, after that, nothing seemed to matter. We – we did what we were told. We've helped to sell stolen pictures and stolen antiques, we've even driven a burglar away from a house he robbed. It's been just a nightmare of doing things we knew were criminal, but facing disaster if we refused. That – that's what's been happening.'

She stopped again, and after a short silence Dawlish spoke quietly.

'It all sounds very understandable, Eileen, even if it isn't very creditable. You must have known it couldn't go on indefinitely.'

'Oh, we did! But we thought that if we could only wait until the war was over, if we could only be sure there was no danger to Raymond because of the war, and him being a German and a Nazi party member – we could give it up. It's true, I swear it's true!'

Dawlish said: 'I think it is.'

'You – you do?' She leaned forward, her eyes brighter than they had been since he had entered. 'Oh, then, you'll help us, won't you? You must help us!'

'Where I can I will,' said Dawlish.

She clutched impulsively at his arm.

'You can, I'm sure you can. We – we came down here because Colonel Cole told us to. Then – then in the woods this morning he told me that we had to break into the room that – that a man named Prior occupied, and see what we could find.'

'Oh,' said Dawlish.

'We'd never actually done anything before, we'd only helped others to do it – often we didn't know what was happening, we just drove people from place to place, and learned afterwards that a house had been burgled. But – but we did break in, and Raymond found a locked portfolio. It was after that I saw Cole talking to – to a man who put something under the bonnet of your car. I heard him say it would – would finish you. So I followed you. I saw the man do it, and then I waited, and stopped you from driving.'

She broke off. 'That's all,' she said. 'That's all there is, Mr Dawlish.'

'How do you think I can help?' asked Dawlish.

'By not saying anything about us! You're working for the police, aren't you? I heard someone saying you were a special agent – it was all over the hotel this morning. If – if you just believe us, if you don't give Raymond away, that will help us tremendously. And – and we could help you to trace Cole – '

Dawlish smiled drily.

'My dear, if Cole were trapped and he even suspected you had anything to do with it, do you think he would hold his tongue?'

The animation died from her eyes.

'I – I hadn't thought of that.'

'I was afraid you hadn't,' said Dawlish. 'Well, leave it for the time being, and we'll see what can be done. Meanwhile, someone gave me a note in Ringwood High Street this morning – do you know who it was?'

'I don't know anything about it.'

'Someone also pushed a note under my door – do you know about that?'

'No, honestly I don't.'

Dawlish said slowly: 'Were you to do anything else when you went into Prior's room?'

'What do you mean?'

'Did you interfere with a bottle of aspirins, or put anything in a bottle?'

'In a bottle?' She was bewildered. 'Of course not. We just searched the room – or Raymond did. I stood by the door, looking out.'

'I see,' said Dawlish. 'Well, we seem to have cleared the air a little. Now what do you think you'd better do?'

'I – I want to see Raymond.'

'Yes, of course.' Dawlish stood up, and the girl looked into the mirror, running a comb through her hair. Dawlish said suddenly:

'Oh, Eileen – *are* you married?'

He could see her reflection in the mirror, and he saw her colour heighten. She stopped combing for a moment, and then turned towards him.

'Do – do you have to know that?'

Dawlish shrugged: 'Come, it isn't so terrible.'

'We're going to be, as soon as we can, as soon as Raymond feels free. We've never stayed as – as husband and wife before, and Raymond makes up a bed on the settee, he – he's such a darling, you'd never believe it.' She paused, and then said sharply: 'Cole told us to register as Mr and Mrs Black. We wouldn't have done otherwise.'

'Do you know why?'

'No,' said the girl a little helplessly. 'No, I don't know at all. It seems crazy, but we can never be sure what he'll tell us to do next.'

Felicity opened the door, and walked with her along the passage. Dawlish stayed in his room, and looked out of the window. He saw Tim and Black walking across the lawn; Tim was talking animatedly. That was another development that he had not been expecting.

He thought over the girl's story. So many statements stood out that it was difficult to decide which was the most important.

Felicity came in, and closed the door quietly behind her.

'Tim and Black are coming up the stairs,' she said. 'Eileen's in her room. Well, Pat, what do you make of it?'

Dawlish slid both hands in his pockets.

'I don't quite know,' he said. 'It's the most amazing story of naive innocence I've ever heard, or else it's a tissue of lies – very much a tissue, because most of its so thin you can see

98

through it. How serious were you when you asked me not to disbelieve her?'

Felicity said: 'She's only told me about being blackmailed, not about the other.'

'Hmm. Well, what do *you* make of it?'

'I think that she told the truth, said Felicity quietly, '*as far as she sees it.*'

CHAPTER 16

And Timothy Too

Tim Jeremy came in a few minutes afterwards, and they heard from him a story not unlike that which Eileen had related. He had followed Black to his room, and after a sharp exchange of words, he had shown – he said – the mailed fist. Once Black had realised that he was suspect, he had asked Tim to listen to his side of the story. It included the Nazi party element, the blackmailing, the search of Prior's room. It held precisely the same denials as Eileen's – denials of any knowledge of the death of Smith, of the cryptic notes, and other things.

'I'm beggared if I know what to make of it, said Tim blankly. 'He's a convincing cove, Pat. And damn it, I began to like the fellow. He seems to have had the devil of a bad time one way and the other. But how could a man be such a fool? If he'd told the authorities in the first place – well, you know what I mean.'

'Yes,' said Dawlish, 'I know what you mean. It sounded a hundred per cent sincere, and yet the essentials aren't believable. Well, my bet is that Black is the liar, Eileen the victim. She's in love with the man, and women in love will believe all manner of incredible things. Won't they, darling.'

Felicity said drily. 'Some do, some just pretend to.'

'That's strong language from you,' said Dawlish, 'but it about sums it up. Let's work it out this way: Eileen is playing a part in this affair which helps Cole and Black – she's their cover, or Black's cover. A young couple, very much in love, always travelling about together – the type of thing that appeals to the romantic of every age.'

'But why couldn't Black tell her the truth?' Tim said.

'My dear oaf, she wouldn't believe the truth. Her Raymond is a victim, pure as the driven snow, ill-treated by circumstances and vicious international laws. He plays his part, he says, with utmost honesty, except this farrago of nonsense about being a member of the Nazi Party. That, says he, he keeps from the police, and at all costs they must be prevented from knowing it. Along comes Cole, with his knowledge. Black appears to obey orders unwillingly, Eileen obeys them, only for Black. She probably knows nothing about the espionage tie-up – *if* there is one.'

'What else could it be?' asked Tim.

'The robbery motive's a strong one. But according to Prior, there's no doubt about the espionage, and so we'll take that on its face value. Meanwhile, we don't quite know where we are, and I think a trip to town is indicated.'

'Tonight?' asked Felicity.

'Yes, darling, and not with you. You and Tim will stay here and keep your weather eyes open for any developments. Meanwhile I'll see Morely. We can't go on without a fuller knowledge of the set-up, and we certainly aren't likely to learn anything from Prior at the moment.'

'Who do you think poisoned Prior?' asked Felicity.

'Black could have worked it with the aspirins,' said Dawlish, 'but Black couldn't have slipped that note under my door – he was with Eileen in the grounds.'

'Well I'm damned!' exclaimed Timothy.

'So – there's someone else,' said Felicity. 'In the hotel, I mean.'

Dawlish nodded, for to him that seemed the first and most important thing; that there was someone else in the hotel who could have operated against Prior, and who had sent him the message: '*First Smith, second Prior, third – why not Dawlish?*'

That thought lingered in his mind a long time as he sped along the road to London. All he had in his grasp were a number of loose ends; he could see neither the beginning or the end of the problem. He did not know for certain what was suspected behind Black's activities and, beyond Black's, Cole's.

He thought again of Eileen's story. In the first place, he was quite sure that no known enemy alien would have been allowed the freedom that Black had been given; the man had lied to Eileen about that. It was almost certain that Black had never disclosed himself as an enemy alien, but had registered as a British national.

That could be checked up.

Dawlish watched the road behind him in the driving mirror, but he was not followed.

He had left the hotel just after six-fifteen; it was eight-thirty when he pulled into the courtyard of Scotland Yard. On the past few miles he had been particularly watchful, for he knew that word could have been telephoned from the Lodge, or near it, for him to be picked up near London and followed.

As far as he could tell, no one had taken any interest in him.

He inquired of a sergeant on duty whether the Assistant Commissioner was in, and he was not surprised to be told 'yes'. For Sir Archibald Morely was a conscientious man.

A year or two more than forty, and young for an Assistant Commissioner, he sat at his desk in a large office overlooking the new wing of the Yard, and smiled a little dourly at the large man who was his cousin.

'Well, Pat – why didn't you tell me you were coming up?'

'Why don't you offer me a chair?' demanded Dawlish, pulling one to the desk and sitting down. 'And you can manage some sandwiches? I'm famished.'

Morely pressed a bell on his desk, while Dawlish went on:

'Well, now – I didn't telephone because I didn't want to be overheard. I wouldn't like to rely on all the lines at Marsham Lodge being free from interruption. And there are things that can be better talked about.'

He paused when the door opened and a policeman came in. Morely sent him for sandwiches, or whatever he could bring in the way of a cold meal, and when the door closed he looked across at Dawlish, grave-faced and, Dawlish thought, very tired.

'Was Prior all right when you left him?'

Dawlish said: 'Prior, I hope, will live. He certainly isn't likely to work any more on this job.'

Morely leaned forward sharply.

'What happened?'

Dawlish began to explain, but stopped when a tray of food was brought in. Thereafter he talked while he ate, quietly, but with considerable effect. He left nothing out; not even Eileen's story. If there was a way in which he could help her, it was certainly not by keeping anything back from the police.

He had finished when the policeman returned, with beer and two glasses. When the door closed he poured the beer, stood up, and took a glass to Morely's desk.

'Here's luck,' he said. 'Don't look so down in the mouth, man, we're not in Queer Street yet!'

Morely drank slowly, then lowered his glass.

'We're not far off it, Pat. I'll tell you straight out that I don't like the situation. We've had a lot work put in on this business, and we thought that in the Blacks – or Black and this girl, whose real surname is Granger – we were getting near the end of it, not the beginning.'

'You could make the short journey from Black to Cole,' said Dawlish.

'Ye-es. Cole – it's so difficult to believe, and yet I suppose you're right. You've a fiendish habit of being right, haven't you? But Cole – he's one of the live wires of the agricultural development scheme. Are you *quite* sure the man you saw was Cole?'

'I haven't been positively introduced,' said Dawlish, 'but I'll stake my shirt on it.'

'Oh, well, that should be good enough.' Morely opened a drawer and took from it a file, and an envelope. The envelope he handed to Dawlish. 'That's your authority – the Home Secretary sent it over this afternoon. But we were working on the assumption that Prior would be handling the case.'

'It can be altered,' said Dawlish gently.

Morely smiled.

'All right, you beggar! I can see you'll never be happy unless you have a free hand. Why the devil it even entered your head to follow Black I don't know, but you seem to be born for trouble. Well, now, I'll give you a resume of what we know.'

Morely talked for fifteen minutes, without stopping. It was quite clear that he had studied the situation deeply. Inquiries had been left to the police, he said, because they were in a better position to keep a general watch than the Special Branch agents, or Secret Service men who could only be used in small numbers. Far larger numbers were needed for the matter in which Black was involved.

It had started the previous year.

Before he said when or how, Morely confirmed Dawlish's belief that Black had registered as a British National. Not for some time had it been discovered that he was of German birth, and reputedly of Nazi sympathies. He had spent more than half of his life in Germany.

(Very little of what he had told Eileen was true, reflected Dawlish grimly.)

Black's numerous trips about the country, at first brought under suspicion because he was obviously not affected by petrol rationing, had been watched. No petrol evasion charge had been preferred, since Black's journies concerned the south of England exclusively, and were mainly in agricultural districts. By the time that was established, Black's actual nationality had been discovered.

At the same time, complains had been received from farmers in the south of the poor quality of feeding stocks, and of damage to stock which they held in their barns. There was nothing very big, but it was worrying. Small fires had destroyed quantities of oil-cake, scarce enough without 'accidental' destruction. Fires had also started in fields after corn had ripened and was ready for cutting. No single instance was of great importance; but collectively substantial damage had been done.

Morely went on:

'The movements of any man in the part of the country affected was of interest, and the Blacks seemed likely to be concerned. That was little more than guesswork, if you like. At all events, I put Smith and Prior on to them; they're first-class men – or they were,' said Morely slowly. 'They didn't look their part, of course, and that was important. But I'm getting away from the subject. We couldn't get beyond Black. His connection with the trouble seemed certain, although it would be difficult to prove. Fires and other damage – '

'Such as?' interrupted Dawlish.

'During the winter potato stacks were opened to the frost, and big stocks ruined. Stocks of seed were damaged by acid or oil. There is a variety of ways in which it could be done, and on a small scale it has been done. Black couldn't take an active part in all of them; it seemed to us that he was carrying orders, but we couldn't find his contact in London, and we wanted it badly. I told Smith and Prior to keep him and the girl under observation every possible moment while he was at Marsham Lodge.'

Dawlish said grimly: 'Smith did. Someone saw him, poor beggar.'

'Ye-es. And you think Cole actually killed him?'

'It seems likely. And my uniform was taken because it was the right size. I fancy that Cole had no idea at the time that I've been mixed up with you people.' Dawlish grinned.

'It isn't a laughing matter,' said Morely. 'It's damnably serious. More food has been grown in this country this summer and autumn than ever before. Stocks at the farms are enormous. The harvest is either in, or about to be gathered. Potatoes will be up this month. Stringent precautions are being taken, the Home Guard in country districts is keeping strict watch, fire-fighters are organised in the villages as well as the towns, but a tremendous lot of damage can be done by one man. A single match will set a field of corn on fire – I needn't go on, need I?'

Dawlish shook his head. 'Prior mentioned foot-and-mouth disease.'

'Yes. The disease can only too easily be carried from one district to another. You can take it from me that it's worrying the Ministry of Agriculture non stop, but it's one of those damnable things that can't be traced. Prior was trying to get at the heart of it, to stop disaster before it comes. What do you think you can do?'

CHAPTER 17

Meeting of Friends

Morely's last words seemed to echo round the room.

'*What do you think you can do?*'

There was a faint emphasis on the 'you' but that concerned Dawlish less than the actual framing of the question. Morely was not optimistic; Dawlish, who knew his cousin well, imagined that there had been a great deal of work done on the case, and that the results were so discouraging that Morely was beginning to think that disaster – if disaster was not too strong a word – would come before there was any chance of stopping the organisers.

Beyond Black, they had gone no further than Cole – and they would not have reached him, but for a chance walk which Dawlish had taken, in a moment of mild playfulness against the police. Morely had inferred, moreover, that Dawlish's word against Cole would hardly be strong enough to stand. Prior, too, had been reluctant to believe anything against the owner of Ley Manor. Possibly this was due to anxiety lest there should be insufficient evidence against Cole, and – even more important – lest Cole, if arrested, should either 'prove' his innocence, or make it quite clear that he was no more than a cipher in the plot against agriculture.

Was that too definite a way of expressing the situation?

Dawlish thought not. Morely had more than implied that both the Ministry of Agriculture and the police were really perturbed. They feared the wreckage of the results of a year of stupendous effort, and the endangering of a case before its entire completion.

Dawlish said quietly: 'I don't know, Archie, but I can have a darned good try. It's those beyond Cole who are worrying you, of course. Anyhow, for a start I could work on Black, but I think there's a better method.'

'And that is?'

'Through Eileen – what did you say her name was – oh, yes, Granger. Supposing I appear to believe her story absolutely? Supposing Felicity strings along with her, and I make a friend of Raymond Black. They'll think – or Black will think – that he has me where he wants me. He pitched that story to Tim Jeremy in the hope of disarming me, there's no doubt of that. Let him think he's been successful.'

Morely looked dubious.

'It gives us some kind of connection to Cole, through Raymond Black,' Dawlish urged. 'It may take time,' he added, 'and for that I'll need an extension of leave.'

'It's been arranged before, so I suppose it can be again.'

'Good man. And Tim and Ted are on leave at the moment. Not to mention Crummy Wise. Could they get extension, do you think? If three or four of us gather at the Lodge, all jolly good friends on leave together, it will take me out of the spotlight a bit.'

'I can't promise miracles,' said Morely, a little irritably, 'but I'll see what I can do.'

Content with that, Dawlish left the Yard soon afterwards, and went on to the London flat which he shared, when on leave, with Tim Jeremy, and Ted Beresford. Both of them had promised to get to the Lodge for a day or two if it could be arranged. Ted was engaged to be married, and much time was taken up by his fiancée. Tim Jeremy was also engaged, but for him time hung more heavily as his girl was out of the country on a mission connected with the Red Cross. Crummy Wise had no attachments; Crummy, that ingenuous and attractive youngster, might prove a boon. Dawlish let himself into the flat, and contemplated the possibility of Tim, Red, Crummy and himself – with Felicity, of course, but Felicity would look after Eileen Granger –

working as they had worked before on matters of national importance.

Time for thought was obviously needed. Meanwhile he went to his Club, the Carilon, and for some two hours chatted to an elderly member who had an estate in Hampshire and was a member of the Hants Agricultural War Committee. Thus he learned much of Colonel Cole, who, though not a member of the committee, was an enthusiastic co-operator. A great fellow, Cole, it appeared.

Oh, yes, an excellent fellow, Cole.

Dawlish learned other things; that Cole was a widower, and lived at Ley with his only daughter, a middle-aged woman and a semi-invalid. Privately, he had had a sad, rather tragic life, the elderly member said, with growing sentiment.

Dawlish began to be a little weary of Cole's excellence.

'Tell you what, Dawlish. There's an article in *The Countryman* – must be a copy somewhere in this place – Cole wrote it. Gives you a pretty sound idea of what reforms he proposes, and tries to get us to adopt. Working them very well down in our corner of the country, too.'

'Oh, I won't worry now,' said Dawlish, who did not want word of his interest to get back to Colonel Cole. 'I'm staying at Marsham Lodge at the moment, and heard of him there.'

'Eh? Oh, the Lodge, yes. Old Marsham used to own it. Great pity he died without issue – good family, the Marshams. Oh, well, young fellow, it's getting near my bed-time.' The member pulled himself from his chair and went off, a white-headed, rather bent man, full of good intentions and enthusiasm.

Dawlish hunted round for *The Countryman*, found it, and turned to the article mentioned. With joy he noted that it was flanked by a profile photograph of Colonel Cole.

He no longer had the slightest doubt about the identity of the man in the brown suit. Cole *had* been a party to that sharp-shooting.

He went back to the flat much encouraged by this confirmation.

The next morning, having bathed, shaved, and breakfasted, he telephoned Beresford and Wise, and arranged to meet them at eleven o'clock at the Carilon. That left him time for another visit to Morely.

Permission had already come through for the four men to have extended leave.

Morely smiled a little grimly.

'They're thinking of your past, old man.'

'I'm thinking of my future,' said Dawlish. 'If this affair blows up, some very startling things are going to happen. What's the arrangement with the Home Guard?'

'They're on regular patrol. I'll give you a note to the Regional Commander.'

'Good man. I suppose nothing's developed over night?'

'I hope not!' said Morely fervently.

Dawlish telephoned the Lodge. Felicity was clearly relieved to hear him, and she confirmed that there had been a quiet night. Dawlish rang off, wondering why he had feared otherwise. He was a little too ready to get scared, he told himself, and he thought as he walked from the Yard to the Carilon Club that the reason was not hard to find.

So little was known; which left the imagination too wide a scope. Mystery and uncertainty, the suspense of waiting for an unknown development, were all more worrying than action itself. He would gladly have plunged into a whirl of free-fighting and physical endurance, knowing that once it came to that, the other side would have already reached the point of desperation.

Apparently they were doing nothing of the kind.

But they were not inactive; he had proof of this when he reached Pall Mall. It was ten to eleven, and he doubted whether either of the others would be early or, indeed, on time for the meeting. So he strolled past the entrance of the Carilon and then walked back again. A dozen cars passed along the Mall, no more. He saw them idly, not seriously thinking that he might be attacked there – in fact the lull had made him a little over-confident.

He heard what he thought was a back-fire – and then, suddenly, a shower of granite chippings from the nearby wall were flung in his face. A second crack was unpleasantly close.

Dawlish dropped flat.

He could not see where the shooting was coming from, for when he tried to open his eyes tears filled them, as the dust from the granite chippings grated against the lids.

He heard shouts.

He heard more, for there was a sharper report, close to him, and then followed the screeching of tyres on the road. He was not hurt – that was something. Another shot, the roar he thought of an army revolver, more screeching, and then from close at hand an inelegant exclamation, and a hearty curse in a different voice.

'The beggar got away,' cried the man who cursed. 'Are you all right, Pat?'

It was Crummy Wise and Ted Beresford. It transpired that they had met in Piccadilly, and walked together to the Carilon.

Then they had heard the shooting, and seen the small car from which the shots had come. Being on foot they had not been able to give chase, although Beresford had fired twice and struck the windscreen at least once. A policeman had taken the number, and the search would be well on by now, Beresford said reassuringly. What Dawlish needed to do was to bathe his eyes.

Slowly, however, his vision was clearing, enough, anyhow for him to see a Daimler car draw up outside the Carilon.

The man who got out of it, and walked into the Club, was Colonel Cole.

CHAPTER 18

Action in London

Both Beresford and Wise were looking towards Dawlish, their backs turned towards Cole.

'Look this way!' urged Dawlish.

Beresford, incredible though it seemed, was a larger man than Dawlish, dark and curly-haired, with an ugly but homely face. Quick moving but slow-thinking, he had for Dawlish a liking which had been born twenty years before; the friendship of Tim Jeremy had dated from the same time and the same school.

Crummy Wise, of a younger generation, eyed Dawlish in surprise.

'What on earth's bitten you?'

'Just at the moment I don't want the gentleman who went in the Club to know that we're acquainted,' said Dawlish. 'So we'll postpone our talk for the time being. After due thanks for your defence work, Ted!' He grinned 'But wait a moment; you're both on extended leave, my sons, and soon to be in hot pursuit of the man you put me on to, Crummy.'

'*What!*'

'No joking,' said Dawlish solemnly.

'Oh, crumbs! And I had a date – '

'No dates from now on. Steel yourself. And don't look towards the Club, idiot! A Colonel Cole just went in – you should locate him without much trouble. Your job, Crummy. Tall, red-faced, strong profile – get a steward to identify him if you have any trouble, but make sure it's one who won't talk.'

'But what – '

'Just keep an eye on him, and report his movements,' said Dawlish. 'Particularly report who sees him at the Club. If you can stop him from realising that you're interested, fine.'

Beresford broke in:

'Hadn't I better handle it, Pat? Crummy's not so – '

'You be blowed,' said Wise with vehemence. 'If I can't tackle a simple job like that I'll know the reason why.' His eyes were shining, for he was a youth with a vivid imagination. 'And it's part of the shooting show?'

'Yes, a large part.'

'Nice *work!*' declared Crummy Wise. '*Very* nice work.' He meandered off, murmuring: 'And I don't know you two, do I? Don't be surprised if I give you a glassy stare.'

He disappeared into the gloomy portals of the club, while Beresford regarded Dawlish with some uncertainty.

'Are you sure he's the right man for it?'

'I don't see why not,' said Dawlish. 'We all started the same way, and he's a bright lad. You're too well known as a friend of mine.'

'All right, have it your own way.'

'Thanks,' murmured Dawlish. 'I'll have a good try! Now we can get into the Club – I don't see any reason why Cole shouldn't see us together. When I've got this grit out of my eyes I'll feel more comfortable, and we can start thinking things out.'

'An excellent idea,' said Beresford. 'At the moment, if I didn't know you better, I'd say you were plain crazy.'

'I take the compliment,' grinned Dawlish.

There was a good chance that in the vast building which was the Carilon, they would not come across Cole unless they looked for him. Certainly they did not see him in the cloak-room, where Dawlish bathed his eyes, nor in a small lounge in which Dawlish explained as much as he thought necessary.

'And so we've had a spot of luck this morning,' said Dawlish. 'Cole might have come here because he knew it was a haunt of mine, but I can't think that's really likely. We must have a break some time. We can follow him about London, and at the end of the day we may have a list of contacts which will be at least useful.'

'Hmm. Are you sure you're on to the right man?'

'Don't let's start *that* again,' said Dawlish vigorously. 'I am *quite* sure that Cole's movements and activities will not bear investigation.'

'That suits me,' said Beresford.

They left the small room, and began a deliberate search for Colonel Cole. Their first clue to his whereabouts came with the sight of Crummy, sitting in the smoking room with his knees crossed, reading the *Times*.

Cole was at the far end. He was talking to two elderly men, one of whom Dawlish recognised as being his white-haired informant of the previous evening. He saw the man turn, and then he knew that his luck had given out, for it was obvious to him that he had been the subject of conversation.

He sauntered across the room, and the elderly member raised a hand.

'You're for it,' muttered Beresford. 'This'll teach you not to be careless when making inquiries.'

Dawlish grunted, and approached the others. Cole regarded him without any great show of interest, and the elderly member said with a smile:

'I'm very glad you've looked in this morning – you'll remember that interesting talk we had about farming? This is Cole – Colonel Cole, Captain Dawlish.'

The two men bowed, a little stiffly.

'It's pleasant to know of your interest, Captain Dawlish.' There was a double meaning in his words, Dawlish knew, or thought he knew.

Dawlish smiled, his expression that of a not particularly intelligent man.

'Always good to know of someone making a big effort these days, sir. Not much of a farmer myself, I'm afraid. See the stuff growing, y'know, but not too sure of the difference between wheat and barley.'

'Townsmen rarely are,' said Cole.

'I – ' began the elderly member, and then broke off. 'Excuse me just a minute, will you? I want a word with Anstruther.' He hurried towards a man of about his own age, and Dawlish introduced Beresford. The three men, all tall and large, made a noticeable sight in the smoking-room; numerous eyes turned towards them.

Dawlish had an unpleasant feeling that the meeting had been engineered. Could that inoffensive man, the elderly member, be part of the organisation which Cole – Dawlish believed – was helping to run? He left the next gambit to Cole.

'So you're staying at the Lodge, Captain Dawlish.'

'Oh, yes. Nice place – everything for comfort and nothing to worry about. Good tennis court, I'm told. Haven't had a chance to use it yet.'

'Haven't you found the murder disturbing?'

That was pretty cool, thought Dawlish. He put on a look of surprise.

'Murder? Oh, yes – news gets about, doesn't it? They collared my uniform, the blighters.'

'Doesn't that make it a little uncomfortable for you?' asked Cole.

'Uncomfortable? The uniform – oh, the police want that. Exhibit A, or something of the kind you know. Sticklers for exhibits, policemen. Or haven't you had much to do with them?'

'Very little,' said Cole. He did not move his reddish-brown eyes from Dawlish's face, and Ted was left entirely out of the conversation. Dawlish believed that in Cole's manner there was unspoken challenge. They were fencing.

'Very sensible of you,' said Dawlish. 'They ask all manner of awkward questions sometimes.'

'I'll take your word for it,' said Cole drily. 'Do you propose to stay at the Lodge long? Under the circumstances, I mean.'

'Oh, I'm not bothered by the murder,' said Dawlish. 'After all, it's not my show.'

'I'm glad you think so,' said Cole.

For the first time Dawlish smiled.

'*Glad*, Colonel? Why?'

Cole looked annoyed with himself; the remark had been careless.

'I was thinking that the local police might resent interference, Captain Dawlish. After all, you have been known to walk where wiser men fear to tread, haven't you?'

'Oh, I don't know,' said Dawlish. 'Wisdom is an arguable point. Most men think they have it. Some actually do.'

A waiter came across the room, and stood at Colonel Cole's elbow. He turned sharply:

'Yes, what is it?'

'A police inspector would like a word with Captain Dawlish, sir.'

'Oh – I'll come out,' said Dawlish. 'The fellow probably wants to know about a shindy outside just before you arrived. Quite a business – some idiot took a pot-shot at me. Off the mark, as it turned out. Luck, I suppose.'

'I hope you don't rely too much on it,' said Cole.

'Only an ass would do that,' said Dawlish flippantly. 'Take the murderer at the Lodge, for instance. Look at the luck he thinks he had! Nevertheless, the police are now bang on his tail! Well, it's no good gossiping here, I shall have to run. Good-morning, sir. I may see something of you at the Lodge.'

'Good-morning,' said Cole impassively, 'it is possible.'

Safely out of the room Beresford gave a low whistle.

'A tough customer, Patrick!'

'He's all that,' admitted Dawlish. 'An interesting beggar. Warnings flying from left to right and from right to left! The air was positively sparking.' He walked on in silence for some minutes, deep in thought. Then: 'I wonder what this policeman does want?'

The call concerned the shooting incident. The car had been found abandoned at Victoria. The Inspector, a man Dawlish did not know, hoped that there was some chance of getting a good description of the driver, but he went away unrewarded. He took up half-an-hour of Dawlish's time, and when Dawlish and Beresford returned to the Club, there was no trace of Cole, nor of Wise.

'Crummy's apparently hot on the trail,' said Beresford.

'Well, we'd better get to the flat, he'll get word through there if he has to contact us,' said Dawlish. 'We'll take a cab, I think.' He was a little on edge during the journey, and for the next hour. There was no word from Crummy, and Beresford told his friend in no uncertain terms that he thought he was an idiot to get worked up over it. Dawlish agreed blandly, but remained on edge, twice going to the window and looking out into the street. He took the precaution of keeping close to the wall as he did so, and Beresford asked:

'Do you expect 'em to take another pot at you?'

'I wouldn't be surprised,' admitted Dawlish. 'We were followed, of course. We're being watched all right. Yes,' he went on as Beresford looked his surprise. 'From the Club door to here we were followed, and that's what's on my mind. Was Crummy tailed too? And if he was, would he have the nous to see it? I'm inclined to wish I'd given you that job after all.'

'I told you – ' began Beresford.

What he had intended to say was lost in the sharp ringing of the telephone bell. Dawlish shot a hand out towards the instrument and lifted it quickly.

'Ringwood Hampshire calling you, sir – hold on please.'

'The Lodge, I fancy,' said Dawlish quietly, and then both men waited for the call to come through.

Both thought of Felicity.

CHAPTER 19

Wider Activity

The call took a long time to come through. Buzzing on the line, occasional snatches of other people's conversation, and twice the operator's: 'hold on, please,' filled the interval. Then at last: 'You're through, go ahead please,' and he heard Felicity's voice.

In it was a note of anxiety which Dawlish was quick to recognise. 'Pat, Tim and Black went out last night, and they haven't come back. There's no word from either of them. Eileen is pretty well frantic. Have you heard from them?'

'Not a thing,' said Dawlish. 'What time did they go?'

'Just after eleven.'

'Together?'

'In a way, yes. We were all four having coffee in the lounge. Then Black said he would like a stroll. Apparently he always has one last thing at night. After he'd gone, Tim perked up and said he'd join him. That's the last we saw or heard of either of them. What do you suggest I do?'

'Just sit tight and persuade Eileen to do the same,' said Dawlish. 'If we take it on its surface value, it looks as if Tim's in a spot, but he'll get out of it. How have things been going, apart from that?'

'We-ll – ' Felicity laughed a little uncertainly. 'Darling, you won't approve, but do you know I'm beginning to *like* Black.'

'Great Scott!' exclaimed Dawlish blankly.

'It's quite true. Once he forgets to be stiff and formal he's rather nice. And he *is* a dress designer– he didn't make that up. I've seen the photographs of some of his models.'

'Well, that seems to clinch it,' said Dawlish, laughing. 'But how do you mean, "rather nice"?'

'You know how different Eileen seemed after we talked to her? Well, something in the same way. The man-of-the-world pose drops away, and he's young and ingenuous. Of course he may be putting it on.'

'That had occurred to me,' said Dawlish a trifle drily. 'I take it you're worried that both Black and Tim met trouble.'

'It does seem possible.'

Dawlish said slowly. 'All right, darling, sit tight and wait for me.'

'When will you be down?'

'Before nightfall, all being well. Ted, Tim and Crummy are all in this until the show's over, by the way. Oh, yes – there's one thing you can do. Try to keep an eye on Cole's place. Have a word with Lockwood if he's at the Lodge today, and ask him to help. One or two Home Guards, out of sight but watching, would do the trick. If there's any query Lockwood can cover it until I'm down, I think.'

'I'll do that,' promised Felicity.

'Fine! I'm interested in comings and goings, but I don't expect anything much to happen.'

'Well don't worry about me, darling, I'm all right. But watch your step.'

She rang off, and Dawlish gave the others a brief resume of what had been said.

'This new side of Black has its interest,' he added. 'I wonder if we can all be making an outsize in mistakes? I wonder – ' he frowned, 'I wonder just what *is* Cole's game, and how much of the blackmailing story is true? I wonder how many of these stories of robbery and burglary have foundation in fact?' He leaned on the corner of the desk a little moodily, and lapsed into silence.

'Perhaps you'll tell us what's on your mind,' suggested Beresford.

'I can't fathom it out,' said Dawlish. 'Complications we can deal with. It's the odd little things which don't fit in anywhere, and are out of character with the general scheme as Morely and the Ministry see it, that are the trouble. Eileen and Black start off being a brace of spies – that's what we thought, at all events – and they gradually develop into a rather frightened, naive and not unlikeable couple. Felicity's judgment's sound enough; if she can see a better side of Black, it's there.'

'I suppose so,' said Ted.

'We know so,' corrected Dawlish. 'Well, I suppose it will work out, but it's taking some understanding. I shall be glad when we get word from Tim and Crummy. But for the time being the merchant outside is our problem.'

Dawlish stepped to the window again, and carefully screened, looked out. Beresford peered over his shoulder, saw a small car pulled up on the other side of the road. The man at the wheel was reading a newspaper, and seemed immersed in it.

'Slip downstairs and walk past him,' said Dawlish. 'Get some cigarettes, or anything you need, and then come back. We'll check up on the gentleman.'

Beresford agreed, and as he sauntered down the street, the man left his car, with a casual air which Dawlish, watching from the flat, found amusing. He walked on the other side of the road a few yards behind Beresford, and on the latter's return journey he retraced his steps, although so casually and looking about him with such boredom that Beresford himself admitted he would have noticed nothing had he not been on the look out for it.

'Now you're sure of him, what are you going to do?' Beresford demanded.

'I think we'll get him up here,' Dawlish suggested. 'I'll go out, and you go out also, but by the back way. I'll give you a five minutes start, and we'll have him between us.' His eyes were bright at the thought of action, brighter when he reached Brook Street and sauntered across the road to the small car. The man had climbed out. Dawlish reached him, and stood by the open door. The man had his right hand on it. He was nondescript-looking individual, the type of man one would put down as a solicitor's clerk, or something equally respectable. He appeared now, to be a little frightened.

'Good-morning,' Dawlish said pleasantly.

There was a muttered response.

'What can I do for you?'

'I – er – don't understand,' said the nondescript one, hesitantly. He looked over his shoulder and saw Ted not ten yards away.

At once he made an instinctive movement towards the driving-seat. Dawlish put out a hand and gripped his wrist.

'I shouldn't – we want a chat, don't we? After all, you sought the interview.' He tightened his grip, and the man came away from the car. He came reluctantly, yet clearly not prepared to make much of a fight.

'This – this is outrageous – '

Beresford had joined them, and they walked across the road, leaving the car where it was but taking the ignition key and locking the doors. Throughout these operations the man watched nervously. Now he walked between them, dragging his feet.

'I – I insist on knowing what this is about!'

'That's precisely what we're going to tell you,' said Dawlish. 'Upstairs, little man.'

Reluctantly the man went upstairs. Dawlish's flat was on the first floor, and Beresford had a key. He started to put it in the lock when the man's manner changed abruptly. In one swift movement he jabbed a pen-knife, concealed in his left hand, into Dawlish's wrist. The jab did no serious damage, but it made Dawlish relax his grip.

The prisoner pulled himself free, and pounded down the stairs. He would certainly have reached the street had not a resident of the flats turned into the main entrance at that moment. During the momentary stuffle, Dawlish caught up with him.

The resident stared wide-eyed.

'What on earth – '

Dawlish was startled then, for their escaped prisoner released a left swing which, had he, Dawlish, not dodged in time, would have shaken him badly. A straight right brushed against his chin, and a kick towards his stomach might have had a telling effect but for the fact that he shot out his hand and caught the man's ankle. Even then he did not succeed in pulling his opponent entirely off balance; the fellow had the springiness of an eel. He wrenched his ankle away, and then let loose a piledriver for the solar plexus.

Dawlish blocked the punch, and then loosed a left which went right home.

Behind Dawlish stood Beresford, while behind his opponent teetered the resident, a middle-aged man still staring incredulously, and yet making no attempt to go away. Actually it happened so quickly that he had little time to adjust himself to what was taking place.

Dawlish evaded another straight left, and then sent home a right with more force than any of his earlier blows. It sent the man staggering backwards, and left him wide open for a clip to the chin which pushed the other sideways.

Dawlish gripped his wrists in one hand, and turned towards the stairs again. The man was beyond resisting any further.

'Apologise to the resident,' Dawlish said to Beresford, 'and tell him we found this beggar tampering with a front door. Up!' He added in a louder voice, and urged his prisoner up the stairs again.

He was pale-faced and breathing hard. His bowler hat had been knocked from his head, and Beresford was bringing it in their wake, after making mendacious explanations to the resident. Again Beresford took out his key and pushed it into the lock, while Dawlish eyed their captive curiously.

He did not look like a fighter, but against a man of his own weight he would have put up a good show. He *had* been game. Dawlish was wondering whether a man with such obvious physical courage, for he had not hesitated to risk a scrap with two heavyweights, could be easily persuaded to talk.

Beresford turned the lock, and pushed the door open.

'After you,' he said.

'After you,' said Dawlish in turn, and he urged his prisoner forward. He went into the room and Beresford followed, pushing the door behind him. As it closed there was a movement from the bath-room, and Dawlish saw the ferrety-faced friend of Colonel Cole slowly emerging. He held a small air-pistol in his hand.

That was not all; Cole himself came from behind him.

CHAPTER 20

Gloves Off

Dawlish kept quite still.

Beresford moved his right hand, but as he did so the ferrety man snapped:

'Stop that!'

Beresford had the good sense to obey, and for some seconds there was a complete silence in the room. Then the prisoner shook himself free from Dawlish's grip and turned to Cole.

'I'm glad I gave you good time, Colonel.'

'Very good time, Drew, thank you.' Cole was smiling, but only with his lips. His cold eye lighted on Dawlish. 'I do beg you, Captain Dawlish, not to be foolish enough to reach for your gun. These little things – ' he slipped an air-pistol into sight – 'are quite deadly.'

'Most things are deadly against a sitting bird,' said Dawlish. He stepped to a chair and sat down, entirely oblivious of men and guns. 'Well, well, well! Of all the born fools, we're the worst, Ted. We walked right into it.'

'Into what?' asked Beresford, mystified.

'Into one of the oldest and corniest traps on record,' went on Dawlish. 'Lured from the flat while the Colonel and his mobster slip into the back door.'

Cole said sharply:

'You have a quick appreciation, Captain Dawlish – I hope you pick up other things as quickly.'

Dawlish eyed him blandly.

'But certainly. I am particularly noted for the unerring instinct with which I can scent a villain!'

'We have had quite enough of your peculiar brand of humour,' said Cole sharply. 'Dawlish, I did not come here to bandy words, I came to make sure that you don't interfere any further in this affair. It has nothing to do with you, and you'll only get yourself hurt if you continue.'

Dawlish drawled: 'You think so?'

'Lemme kick his teeth in,' pleaded the ferrety one.

'Let him try,' said Dawlish. 'It should be an interesting spectacle. Who thought of this little trick, Colonel?'

'I did.'

'Well, well, well. It's hard to believe that a man of guile could also be so simple. Do you seriously mean to tell me that you think a warning, issued by you to me, will succeed? Don't you think there's been evidence enough already that you're not only at the end of your little caper, but just about ready for the long drop? Didn't it occur to you that I'd been in this show a long, long time before you ever dreamed you'd been spotted –'

Cole interrupted sharply.

'If you're trying to frighten me, you won't succeed. I took the trouble of finding out when you left your regiment, Dawlish, and that was only three days ago. You haven't had time to do more than make yourself a thorough nuisance. I hope a warning will be effective.'

'Well, you're wrong in one,' said Dawlish bluntly.

'Then it will be the more unfortunate for you,' said Cole. 'I hoped to find you more amenable. Perhaps it will persuade you if I tell you that your friend Wise will die very quickly unless you change your mind. I needn't mention Miss Deverall, need I?'

Dawlish said sharply: 'No, you needn't.'

'Ah. Touched at last. So I am sure we can reach an understanding. You have no reason to interfere in my affairs, and there is no reason at all why you should not enjoy a spell of leave, rejoin your regiment, and forget that you were ever unfortunate enough to become a little too meddlesome.'

Dawlish looked at him thoughtfully.

'For your information Captain Dawlish,' Cole went on. 'I had heard of you, and as soon as you arrived at the Lodge I took certain steps. I had to kill Smith, who was proving a nuisance, and it was unfortunate that the police, a little less thick-headed than usual, allowed you to be free instead of detaining you on suspicion for a day or two – for the period of your leave, in fact. That was really all I wanted.'

Dawlish said nothing, and Cole, a little uncertainly, went on:

'How pleasant if those days of leave still left to you Dawlish, were spent in tennis and golf, perhaps even a little riding. All, of course, in the company of Miss Deverall and your charming friends.'

Dawlish stared at him.

'I should so dislike,' Cole went on, 'to shorten the life of so enterprising a young man. Don't pursue your inquiries any further, Dawlish. Smith cannot help you, and I don't think Prior will be able to talk for a long time to come. Just return to the Lodge, collect your belongings, and go somewhere else. That isn't too much to ask, surely?'

Dawlish said: 'I could pretend to do all of those things, or hadn't you thought of that?'

Cole laughed. 'Oh yes, I've thought of it. And for that reason I propose to hold your friend Wise. And I feel quite sure it would depress you greatly if anything happened to him. As soon as your leave is up, then Wise would be released. It is quite simple, really. You do understand, don't you?'

Dawlish said: 'Oh yes. I understand you, but you, least of any man, should not feel complimented by that.'

He believed that Cole thought he was primarily concerned for Crummy Wise; whereas he was not. He knew that the issues at stake were far greater than personal ones, and he knew also *that Cole did not suspect that he had any official rating.*

Cole's voice became a little sharper. 'I gather that Black and his lady have told you of their unfortunate indiscretions. If it will set your mind at rest, I won't require their services much longer. Possibly no longer than the rest of your leave.

Your concern for them does you credit Captain Dawlish, but you see how unnecessary it was.' .

'Is that so,' murmured Dawlish.

'Let me make the situation a little clearer,' said Cole. 'That naive young couple fell into difficulties of their own making, and I took advantage of it. They are really not worthy of your help. They are certainly not worth risking your lives for – and when I say "lives" I mean Miss Deverall's as well, of course.'

Dawlish said pleasantly:

'What a revealing little narration, Colonel. I'm *almost* persuaded – but understand this, and don't forget it. I'll see that couple free before I've finished, if I – or much more likely, *you* – die for it.'

Cole said thinly:

'Dawlish, you are right about one thing. Your life *is* in the balance. I might say it is hanging by a thread. If you decide to go away, I will forget the nuisance you have made of yourself. If you don't – well, *this* will make sure that you don't be a nuisance in the future.'

'This' was the gun that he lifted an inch.

Dawlish said: 'Don't be a fool. Do you think I let this happen without taking precautions? You knew Beresford, Wise and myself – you saw us all at the Carilon together, and your little gunman of the car could identify us. There are others, back and front. You were seen to come in – '

He paused, and Cole tightened his lips.

'*Lemme* kick his teeth in,' said the ferrety-faced man pleadingly. 'He's lyin', Guv'.'

'There was no one at the front,' said the man named Drew.

' 'Corse there weren't. And there weren't no one at the back, I was watching all the time,' said the little man. 'Lemme – '

'You really can't bluff *me*, Dawlish,' said Cole. 'I – '

And then he stopped, for there was a sharp knock on the front door of the flat, followed by the ringing of the bell.

*

The ringing and the knocking faded.

In silence the five men stared at one another – or more accurately, Dawlish and Beresford returned the stares of the trio. Dawlish had never been so relieved in his life as when he had heard the bell ring. He had no idea who it was, and he did not greatly care, but if he had arranged it himself it could not have been timed to greater advantage.

Cole broke the silence.

'Who is that?'

'It might be one of four,' said Dawlish. 'I told them not to wait for me more than twenty minutes or so.' The bell rang again.

Cole turned sharply to his henchmen. 'Open the door, and bring them in.'

'It won't do you any good,' said Dawlish.

'You keep quiet!' Cole's gun covered Dawlish and Beresford, while Drew stepped to the door and the man with the gun stood close to the wall, ready to cover whoever stood there. Dawlish held his breath. Beresford's muscles were tensed. Drew put a hand to the latch, and turned it.

The door opened slowly.

Quickly Dawlish cried out:

'Get away, whoever it is! Tell the police that Cole, of Ley Manor – '

'*You* – ' began Cole, and he squeezed the trigger of his air-pistol. Dawlish ducked, and a bullet hummed an inch or so over his head. There was a shout at the door, and then hurried footsteps. Cole, startled by Dawlish's movement, could not stop Beresford lunging forward and pushing him against the wall. The ferret-faced man turned from the door to meet this new threat, while Drew disappeared, in hot pursuit of whoever was outside.

By then Dawlish had reached Cole. Before he had time to use his gun again Dawlish hit out with such force that Cole's head jerked back, cracking against the wall with a sickening thud. Dawlish left Beresford to deal with the ferrety one, while he dashed out in the wake of Drew and the caller. He could hear the thud of footsteps in the hall below, and he went down the stairs three at a time. He heard a sharp exclamation, and then the slamming of a door. When he reached the hall, he saw a man stretched out across the doorway.

So eager was Dawlish to get outside and find Drew, that he did not look twice until he heard a voice which had a familiar ring calling his name.

'Dawlish – Dawlish – '

Then he looked down, and he saw that the man on the floor was Raymond Black.

CHAPTER 21

Not So Good

He did not know whether Black was merely winded or really hurt, but at that moment he decided that catching Drew was more important than going to Black's aid. He cried out:

'I'll be with you in a moment!' and then rushed for the street. He was in time to see Drew running at speed, and Dawlish, tucking his elbows into his sides, gave chase.

At the end of Brook Street Dawlish stopped, breathing heavily. There were full two hundred people in sight. Those near him looked at him curiously, those farther away, shrugged their shoulders, and passed on.

There was no sense in asking questions, for Dawlish knew well enough that Drew must, by now, have boarded a taxi. That was less important than it would have been had Cole and the ferrety-man not been at the flat. Dawlish comforted himself with the assurance that Beresford would handle them comfortably, and went back towards the flat more leisurely.

Before he talked to Morely, or called in help, he wanted to measure up the situation. Cole had thought he would relinquish the job – Cole, then, did not know much about him. Cole presumably had no idea that Prior had talked, or that he, Dawlish, had been to the Yard on the previous evening. He and Beresford had been followed from the Club, certainly, but it was reasonable to assume that that had been the starting point.

Not so bad, thought Dawlish, though he was still incensed at the ease which which he had fallen into Cole's trap. However, it had turned out more fortunately than he deserved.

Thanks to Black.

Of course, there might have been another way out; Dawlish had been prepared to fight for it, and he had not seriously thought that he and Ted would be given their *quietus*. But it had been a bad enough spell, and he owned much to Black's unexpected arrival.

He could find out the reason for it later.

Black had sounded urgent, too. Dawlish lengthened his stride, suddenly afraid that he had done the wrong thing, and that he should have seen Black before chasing after Drew.

No one was outside the flats.

That surprised him, for he had expected a small crowd. Surely the racing down the stairs, and the earlier fight, had attracted attention. He found that it had, inside the building, for two men and a woman were bending over Black. The man was conscious, and he started up when he saw Dawlish.

'All right, old man,' said Dawlish, and then to the three residents: 'I think everything will be all right now.' He smiled into the three faces, set in excitement rather than consternation: that was one advantage of having a reputation. One of his neighbours had once confided that she looked forward eagerly to his return on leave – things were so quiet when he was away.

Dawlish helped Black to his feet, while the others watched them going up the stairs. It appeared that Drew had simply kicked Black in the stomach, but with a force which had temporarily robbed him of every sensation but pain. The effect of it would not last long, and that was a thing to be thankful for.

The flat door was shut.

'Ted's being careful,' Dawlish said half to himself, and he opened the door with his own key. Then stared into the room with alarm.

All was not well.

It was a shock, so that for a moment he stood absolutely still. He was afraid for Beresford, for Beresford was stretched out on the floor, an ugly wound in his temple. Beneath him was the little man, unconscious also, but holding in his right

131

hand a small piece of iron-piping. The breath must have been forced from his body when Beresford had fallen on him.

There was no sign of Colonel Cole.

*

Dawlish had Beresford on the couch in a few minutes, and saw with infinite relief that the wound in the temple was nothing like as bad as it looked. Obviously the ferrety-one had struck him a glancing blow with the iron-piping. Beresford, as he lost consciousness, had lunged forward, and his great bulk had crushed the smaller man, a bump on the back of his head indicating that he had fallen on the sharp corner of a chair. That helped to explain much of what had happened, and twenty minutes later Beresford confirmed it. The large man was sitting up, with a towel wrapped about his head, drinking tea laced with whisky.

He was not pleased with himself, while Dawlish on the other hand, judged things more cheerfully.

'It can't be helped, and we did get away with our lives,' he pointed out. 'Cole has had a severe shake-up, he's lost at least one of his boy-friends, and we shall recognise Drew in future. On a reckoning, the advantage is with us. But whether it would have been without your arrival, Black, I don't know.'

Black gave a wintry smile.

Tea, laced as was Beresford's, had done much to restore his colour. Dawlish had a peculiar feeling that he was looking at a man he had never seen before. He could understand what Felicity had meant, for about the man who had given so strange and unpleasant an impression on first acquaintance there was a naivete which was almost boyish.

'I'm glad to have been of help, Dawlish. I felt that I had to have a word with you, and when I learned you had come to London, I followed. It's rather a long story.'

'There should be plenty of time,' said Dawlish, 'but before we start it, I'll check up at the Lodge.' He put through a call, and learned that Felicity was in her room, with Eileen. Eileen was still worried out of her wits.

'Tell her she needn't be,' said Dawlish. 'Black's here, and quite unhurt. I haven't seen anything of Tim yet, but I'm hoping he's about. Have you seen Lockwood?'

'Yes – he's off-duty today,' Felicity told him. 'He's doing everything that needs doing, and Cole's place is being watched.'

'Nice work,' said Dawlish. 'And now, my sweet, a final word. Take particular care of yourself and Eileen. Don't go far from the Lodge, and if you go anywhere from it, have Lockwood or some of the other men with you. All clear?'

'All clear,' said Felicity. 'What's been happening at your end?'

'I still hope to be down tonight, and then I'll tell you all about it,' said Dawlish.

When he replaced the receiver he felt more satisfied with the trend of events. Cole's escape was the only black mark – his and Drew's of course. But this set-back was nothing, really, compared with the fortuitous arrival of Black. Dawlish wanted to hear Black's story quickly, but he also wanted word from Tim Jeremy, who should have been on Black's heels.

Black's story came first.

He started off with a statement which Dawlish might well have found disarming.

'Look here, Dawlish, I think you should know everything – I've kept rather a lot back, one way and another.'

Dawlish nodded.

'Well, it's like this. I'm as English as any man, or I feel it. But I didn't let the police know I was a German national. I told Eileen I had, because – well, I thought it would make it easier for her.'

'And for you,' Dawlish said drily.

Black coloured.

'I know. I must seem a pretty awful swine in some ways, but – Cole's got me scared.' His voice rose a little, and Dawlish could see a fine dew of perspiration on his upper-lip. 'At first all I was worried about was keeping my nationality secret. Then Cole got hold of the truth, and forced me into doing some odd things. I didn't think a lot about it, I was too concerned with my own skin. Eileen came with me once or twice, at first – and then before we knew where we were, this fellow had been murdered at an inn where we were staying, and Cole had us both where he wanted us. If – if it hadn't been for the fact that Eileen could have been made to look an accessory in the murder, I would have taken a chance, and told the police about the other business. But I couldn't – it had gone too far. You can see that, can't you?'

Dawlish nodded.

He could not decide how much of what the other said was the truth. On the surface it was plausible enough, but plausibility did not necessarily prove things to be true. He kept an open mind, but he also felt something of Felicity's liking for this new Raymond Black.

'Well – you know pretty well what's happened,' went on Black. 'I told Jeremy, and Eileen told you. We were going to keep it from Cole. I didn't see why he should know we'd told you. I knew that if you were able to get Cole in a corner, you might help us. If you could get him to admit the murder, the other would work itself out. If I have to be interned – well, it won't be for long now, thank God. Hitler can't last for ever.'

'Or so we hope,' said Dawlish.

Black took a deep breath, then went on anxiously: 'Yesterday evening, Cole telephoned me at the Lodge. He – he *knew* what I'd told your friend, what Eileen had told you. Don't say it's impossible – he did know.'

Dawlish stared at him, narrow-eyed.

It was not impossible; he knew that because of the letter pushed under his door. An accomplice other than the Blacks was at Marsham Lodge. An accomplice who could listen-in to conversations, who kept a constant watch and missed very little. Dawlish was running his mind over the guests and the staff, trying to sort the suspects from those quite clearly innocent, and he gave it up only when he realised that he was getting nowhere.

'All right, we'll take it that he knew. What then?'

'He told me to meet him last night – I've had to meet him in the thicket every night at half-past eleven. I went there, but he didn't show up. One of his men did – that fellow,' added Black, and nodded towards the ferret-faced man, who was now in a chair, bound and gagged, and still unconscious.

'Yes,' said Dawlish.

'I was to meet Cole in London. There was a car at my disposal – it was at the end of the Lodge drive. I'm so scared by these swine, Dawlish, that I did what I was told. I reached London about three o'clock. Cole had a flat in Westminster, but when I got there he had gone out. I hung about for an hour, and then went to my own flat, in Jermyn Street. Cole telephoned me there, and told me to go back to the Westminster flat. I did. He kept me waiting for a few more hours – trying to break my nerve, I suppose. He knew that I was getting desperate. He talked about Eileen – in a way that left me no doubt that he was prepared to do absolutely anything to get what he wanted – and then told me that he would give me further instructions today.'

He paused, and Dawlish, looking into the man's tired face, saw the strain in it and believed much of what he said.

'He told me to return to the Lodge,' said Black wearily. 'I started, and got half-way there, and then I turned back.' He put that very simply. 'I've called myself a swine and a coward a thousand times for letting Eileen into this trouble, for not going to the police. I suddenly realised that there *was* a chance of getting her out of it if I told you everything. So, I came back here. I had a bit of engine trouble, and it delayed me, otherwise I would have been here an hour earlier. That's all.'

Dawlish said slowly: 'I'm glad you came back. But you must know more than you've told me about the jobs you've done for Cole. Just what do you do for him?'

Black licked his lips, while Beresford leaned forward. The atmosphere had grown very tense, for both Dawlish and Beresford knew how much depended on Black's story.

If he told the truth.

CHAPTER 22

More Action

Black did not hesitate for long, and when he started to speak, it was in a voice which carried conviction.

'It isn't easy to tell you, Dawlish. But there have been a number of country house burglaries. Chiefly, I've driven one or two men – Drew and Stenner among them – to the house where the burglaries have taken place. Stenner is that fellow's name.' He motioned to the prisoner, who was still unconscious. 'They've gone to the house. I've waited for a bit, and then they've come out carrying stuff in suit-cases. We've then put the suit-cases into the luggage boot and driven off. I think that the idea was that if Eileen and I were seen driving, we wouldn't attract the same notice as two men together.'

He paused, and then went on.

'Once – only once – we went up to the house. I think Cole wanted to make us realise that if we gave him away, we would be up to our necks in it ourselves. If that was the idea, it worked. Then sometimes we drove Drew and Stenner to out-of-the-way farmhouses, and put the stolen stuff in old barns.'

For the first time, Dawlish interrupted.

'How often has that happened?'

'Eight or nine times, I suppose.'

'Would you know the places again?'

'I don't think so. It wasn't possible to see much, and as I said, it was always done at night. There was a clear moon one night, though, and I did recognise the place. It's not far from the Lodge, actually – a little cottage. I've seen it since.'

Dawlish rubbed his chin thoughtfully.

'Would it be Ley Farm Cottage.'

'How the devil did you know that?' Black looked really startled.

'I didn't know, I guessed,' said Dawlish. 'So you deposited stolen stuff at Ley Farm Cottage –'

'Well, at a barn near it.'

'All right, a barn near it, as well as other places. Eight or nine in all, you say. Do you remember any of the houses that have been burgled?'

'No.'

'How could you be sure they were burgled?'

'Well, it stands to reason.' Black frowned in bewilderment. 'I saw the men climb through a window once, as I've said. And they always brought suit-cases away with them. Besides, I've seen reports of the robberies in the papers. You can't doubt *that*.'

Dawlish said thoughtfully:

'It's surprising what you can doubt if you really put your mind to it. If you didn't see the houses, and didn't know their names, how could you be sure they were those named in the burglary when it reached the Press?'

Black stared.

'I – I took it for granted, of course. The places were in the neighbourhood, Hampshire, or Dorset, or close to the borders.'

'Yes,' said Dawlish crisply. 'It works out very nicely. There have been country house burglaries, and when by chance they've been in your neighbourhood, Cole's pointed them out to you. But there's not the slightest proof that you've played any part in them. The burglaries can be, and I think are, quite unconnected with what you've been doing.'

Black half-rose from his chair.

'That *sounds* like nonsense. Dawlish, what do you mean? Cole couldn't have been doing it just to scare Eileen and me!'

Dawlish laughed shortly. 'It certainly isn't a straightforward business. Your big job in the immediate future is to try to remember what places you've visited. Not those of the newspaper reports. If you put your mind to it, you'll recall the vicinities. What towns and villages you passed through, for instance – how far they were from a main road. Get everything you can remember put down on paper. Will you do that?'

'I'll try, but – what is it all about?'

'Leave it for the time being, and I'll tell you,' said Dawlish. 'I've no more than a glimmering of an idea myself yet.' He frowned thoughtfully. 'Just one other thing. Did anyone follow you to London last night?'

'I didn't see anyone.'

'And you've noticed nothing this morning?'

'No, I can't say I have.'

'That's too bad,' said Dawlish, lightly. 'Tim Jeremy left just after you, and should have watched you on your travels. If he did, he made a good job of it, and if he didn't I'll wring his fool neck.'

Beresford said: 'What are you driving at?'

Dawlish beamed.

'If Tim was on Black's tail, and it's heavy odds that he was, then Tim followed either Drew or Cole. It should be a help, and we should hear in the very near future.'

It was not guess-work, it was plain common-sense; and it was vindicated twenty minutes later when the telephone-bell rang, and Tim Jeremy's deep voice sounded over the wires. Tim did not sound excited; he rarely allowed himself to, particularly over the telephone. But he did sound urgent.

'Don't start shooting your mouth off, Pat, I haven't much time here. I'm at a kiosk in Roehampton. Come over Putney Heath on the Roehampton Road, and just before you get to the village you'll see a biggish red house with a high yew hedge – you can't miss it. I followed a cove from the flat, and he's gone to roost there. What's more, Cole followed. Make it snappy.'

And Timothy Jeremy rang off.

*

The problem, as Dawlish saw it, was to decide how much the authorities should know of the morning's developments. He could not yet see whether it would be wise to hand Cole over to the police. It was a course that the Yard would almost certainly insist on, if he should call on their help.

He had been blamed often in the past for taking too much on himself; and he smiled a little ruefully as he thought that he would probably be blamed again that day, for after five minutes' thought he decided that for the time being he would keep what he knew to himself.

Black presented a problem.

The man might have told all the truth; but on the other hand, he might well have been planted on him, Dawlish, in the fifth column way. His story was certainly plausible, and in some ways so odd that it was surely too fantastic to be a lie; but Dawlish wanted to take nothing on chance.

He solved the problem quickly enough.

He telephoned the Yard, and arranged for a special watch to be kept on the flat. He told Black that he wanted to make sure that no one came in while he – and Stenner – stayed there. And he delayed his start for Roehampton long enough to tell the plainclothes men when they arrived, that they were to prevent anyone from coming out, as well as prevent anyone from going in.

These instructions were accepted without question.

'And that's just another reason for thinking that Morely and those men of the Ministry of Agriculture who are getting really worried are prepared to give me *carte blanche*,' Dawlish said to Beresford.

'I wish we had Tim and Crummy with us,' said Beresford as they stepped into Dawlish's Lagonda.

'Tim will be around, and it won't be the most surprising thing in the world if Crummy's inside the house. We could do with two or three more men certainly, but I don't think Cole's using anything in the way of an army.'

'Why aren't you letting Morely know?'

'I don't really know,' admitted Dawlish. 'We'll call it a hunch and leave it at that.' He drove in silence for some time, and then went on: 'It's more than a hunch, of course. The question is: can Cole lead us anywhere, and if he can, will he do so if the police get him now?'

'In short, it *is* a hunch,' grunted Beresford. 'You mean, don't you, that he's more useful free than a prisoner.'

'Something like that,' said Dawlish amiably. 'Keep your peepers open. It'll be as well that we know if we're followed, so that we can do something about it before we get to Roehampton.' He drove as far as Chelsea Town Hall, and then Beresford said:

'There is a small car behind.'

'How long's it been there?'

'Since Victoria, or a little before that.'

'We'll go as far as Fulham, and turn up towards Walham Green,' said Dawlish. 'It isn't the quickest way to Putney Heath, but if we go direct the johnny might take it into his head to tele-word that we're on our way.'

The little car continued to follow them. It was a Black Morris 8, and showed, on occasions, a surprising turn of speed. Dawlish drove to Walham Green, slowed down, then stopped at a tobacconist's, and let Beresford out. While he was buying cigarettes Dawlish watched the Morris. Its driver pulled up twenty yards ahead.

Dawlish went on again, and stopped at the junction of Fulham Road and Fulham Palace Road. This time, when he drew up the Morris stopped a little way behind. Dawlish noticed that the driver was a small man, middle-aged, and nondescript.

'He's our man, all right,' said Dawlish. 'We'll cook his goose, I think. Where's the police-station in this part of the world?' He drove on, remembering where there was a station in Hammersmith. Half way along Fulham Palace Road the Morris accelerated, and passed the Lagonda, a piece of impudence which made Dawlish grin.

The Morris drove into a side-turning.

And then a lorry, which had been travelling steadily enough towards them, suddenly altered its course, and increased its speed.

There was no time to evade it.

To passers-by it must have looked as if the lorry skidded. Actually Dawlish saw the driver turn the wheel. The driver must have known that, sitting high up and in a six-ton six-wheeler haulage vehicle he was safe enough. The low-lying Lagonda stood little higher than the lorry's chassis, and the lorry-driver was in little danger.

Dawlish swung his wheel.

The front of the lorry reared up in front of him, and then the crash came. Dawlish had turned just enough to avoid a head-on collision, but not enough to evade the lorry altogether. The latter's offside wheel ripped off the Lagonda's wing, while the impact flung Dawlish and Beresford from their seats. Then the lorry went on, dragging the wreckage of the Lagonda with it, while people cried out, and the wheels of passing cars screeched as their drivers pulled up sharply.

To Dawlish and Beresford, lying bruised and crushed, there seemed no end to it.

CHAPTER 23

Dawlish Goes On

But the lorry stopped at last, and the driver climbed slowly down from his seat. Dawlish eased himself painfully away from Beresford. They looked at each other in shocked silence, until Dawlish, rather gingerly, shook his head.

'It *can't* be true.'

'I'm true all right,' said Beresford. 'Let's see if we're still working.' Cautiously they moved each limb, and turned their heads with slow precision. As they did so, the man in the Morris walked towards them. As quite a crowd of people were doing the same thing, there was nothing surprising in it. Dawlish, still dazed, grew, minute by minute, clearer-headed. He was glad to see a police-sergeant amongst three men in blue who were pushing their way through the crowd.

The lorry-driver was a burly, oafish-looking man, from whose thick lips a cigarette dangled. His eyes were bleary and furtive.

'I skidded,' he said as if aggrieved. 'I couldn't 'elp it, I skidded. Drivin' too many hours, that's wot it is – I come from York since dawn this mornin'.'

'It wasn't your fault.' A sharp voice from the driver of the Morris cut in. 'This man was driving on the wrong side of the road.'

'I *thought* 'e was,' said the driver. 'But I skidded – I don't wanta tell a lie, I skidded. All the hours o' the day an' night driving' – '

Dawlish said crisply:

'I shouldn't worry, driver, you'll soon have a rest. Probably longer than you bargained for.' He turned to the driver of the Morris. 'So you say I was on the wrong side of the road?'

'Yes, I do.'

'Let's get this straight,' said the sergeant. 'I – '

'Here is my card,' said Dawlish, and he handed Morely's pass to the sergeant. Its instructions were simple; any policeman was to take the holder's orders. The man's expression altered. 'All right, sergeant?'

'*Yes*, sir.'

Dawlish raised his voice.

'I am on special work. The lorry was driven at me deliberately, to prevent me carrying it out. This man has followed me from the West End, and twice endeavoured to force me into a collision. Have them both detained for questioning.' He spoke with authority, and, as he expected, his 'special work' silenced any criticism which might have come from the crowd; a crowd would want normally to see fair-play for the lorry driver, but the hint of special activities would swing their sympathy well into Dawlish's favour.

The driver's lips opened, and the cigarette dropped out.

' 'Ere, wot – '

'I've never heard such nonsense!' blustered the little man. He looked from right to left, as if for a way of escape.

Dawlish said clearly:

'Look after them, sergeant. I'll prefer the charges when I get back. But I'll need another car.'

'We can fit you up at the station, sir.' The sergeant gathered his inference, knew that he wanted the 'special work' to be emphasised. 'What is it, sir, more of these ruddy quislings?'

'I think you've a nice brace here,' said Dawlish.

Thus it was that a crowd which might have been friendly grew hostile towards the driver and the little man, who were hustled away in a car commandeered by the sergeant. Another motorist offered to drive Dawlish and Beresford to the station.

'There's one advantage of having a *visa*, as Archie calls it,' Dawlish murmured to Beresford. 'I'll have a word with

143

the Inspector in charge, while you see what you can do about a car.' He hurried into the station, and in five minutes had explained enough to the Inspector in charge to ensure the quick removal of the two prisoners to Cannon Row, as well as for a report to go to the Assistant Commissioner. Beresford, meanwhile, had secured a Wolseley 14, and within twenty-five minutes of the start of the accident, they were on the road again. They were bruised and stiff but not otherwise hurt.

'Cole loses his men one by one,' murmured Dawlish. 'They're smart though, aren't they?'

'And there seems to be a lot of them,' said Ted.

'The more the merrier, my son, and we'll know the worst within half-an-hour.'

They did not speak again until they were within sight of Roehampton village. The big house was easily spotted by the yew hedge which was taller than either Dawlish or Beresford. They drove past at speed, not stopping until, in the High Street, they saw Tim Jeremy sitting at the wheel of his car. From where he was sitting he could see anyone who entered the house.

His thin face was set in lines suggesting exasperated boredom that changed when he recognised Dawlish and Beresford. As they pulled up in front of him, he climbed from his car.

His greeting was fervent but low-pitched. Dawlish noted at once his red-rimmed eyes, evidence of lack of sleep.

He said quietly: 'Who's gone in?'

'No one, since I 'phoned. A couple of men went out, in a small car – a Ford. I've had a word with the local bobby. He told me that the house has been empty for some time, and was let a month ago. Tenant's name, Coleson.'

Dawlish grinned.

'A thin enough cover. Servants?'

'A scratch lot. Two women, an old man, and a girl. Coleson has visitors, but none of them very extraordinary.'

'Two women, an old man, and a girl,' murmured Dawlish. 'Even if we allow for a couple of louts in addition to Cole,

Coleson and Drew, it shouldn't be beyond the three of us. Let's get moving.'

'What have you told the bobby?' asked Ted.

'Nothing of importance,' Tim assured him, 'and he's now on a beat the other side of the village. We should have half-an-hour, as far as I can tell.' They walked together towards the house, which was called – not surprisingly – The Yews. Near the hedge, Dawlish said:

'Ted, find the back exit from the garden, and get in that way. Keep an eye on the back door, once you're in the grounds, and we'll try the front.'

'That suits me,' said Beresford.

He went off, and Dawlish, who had elected Ted to go instead of Tim since the larger man was fresher, went with Jeremy to the green-painted front gates. When they went through, they saw that all the front windows were bricked up – or rather, a brick wall reaching to the top of each window had been built a foot away from them. As blast protection it was probably effective, but it was rather odd to find every window so meticulously guarded.

He glanced upwards.

'Steel shutters too, if I mistake not,' he murmured, 'and half of 'em closed. Mr Coleson doesn't want to be over-looked, does he?'

'It was Cole all right,' said Tim.

In silence they walked to the brick-protected porch, and reached the front door. A huge brass knocker invited their attention.

'Do we knock or ring?' asked Tim.

'We knock and we ring,' said Dawlish, and he did so.

They waited for some minutes. The silence was a strange thing, since they knew that at least two people were in the house, and the policeman had told Tim of four servants.

Dawlish had been almost leisurely in his approach, for he had wanted neither to arouse unwelcome suspicion, nor to attract attention from passers by. But in his mind, and those of his friends, a tension was growing, a feeling that they might have found a place of vital importance. The way in which the rooms were protected from bomb damage also suggested that.

For the fourth time Dawlish knocked and rang. 'And if they don't answer, we'll break in,' he assured Tim.

He thundered long on the door, the vibrations echoing hollowly, but nothing happened beyond that. 'Thanks be for the yew hedge,' Dawlish said crisply. Pulling on a glove, and rounding his fist he broke the glass of one of the side windows.

The splintering noise faded, and silence followed.

Pushing his arm through the hole as far as his shoulder, Dawlish groped for, and found, the bolt of the door. He drew it back, and a moment later they stepped inside a large, ill-lighted hall. The gloom was caused partly by the brick-work outside the porch, and partly by the fact that the rooms on either side, all with their doors standing open, were also darkened.

There was no sound.

'Go through for Ted,' said Dawlish, and he went with his friend alongside the stairs. The passage was a wide one ending at a closed door. The staircase was imposing, larger than might have been expected in a house of that size.

In a few moments, Tim and Ted came back together; all three men appeared rather at a loss. Dawlish rubbed his chin.

'A rum show. I wonder whether we should go upstairs or down? Could they have got out before we arrived?'

Tim shook his head decisively. 'I could see both exits, and the hedge runs right round the house. Cole and Drew went in within ten minutes of each other.'

Dawlish frowned.

'We-ell, we'll know in a few minutes. Ted, hold the fort down here. If you stay in the hall you should be able to keep a weather-eye on the cellar as well as upstairs. We'll go up, Tim, for a start.' He turned towards the stairs, his movements silenced by the thick pile carpet.

Beresford stood half-way along the passage.

'Two floors, judging from the height of the place,' said

Dawlish. 'Keep on the landing, Tim, and I'll explore the rooms here.' He drew his revolver from his pocket as he went forward, along the first of two passages.

He did not know what to expect.

He was oppressed by the silence, and puzzled by its meaning. Twice he had been trapped – or nearly trapped – by a decoy sent by Cole. Drew had proved the decoy once, and the driver of the Morris the second time.

Could this be a refinement of that method?

He inspected three large bedrooms, but they contained no human being. The utter silence of the house seemed to increase; certainly its effect did. He went back to the landing where Tim was standing, a gun in his hand, and looked over the bannisters. Ted was waiting below, alert and watchful.

Dawlish went along the second passage.

The result was the same – precisely *nil*. The only difference in the second inspection was that he found two bedrooms and a library. The furniture in all the rooms was on the same massive, Victorian style. Crossing the library a board creaked behind him, making a report like a pistol shot. Dawlish swung round, then grinned at himself, although he was beginning to sweat at the neck and the forehead.

The whole set-up was uncanny.

He rejoined Tim, and they went together to the next flight of stairs, a narrower one than the first. They were halfway up it, still surrounded by ghostly silence, when the first noise struck their ears. It was Beresford's voice, high-pitched, alarmed.

'Pat, come down! Pat – '

The words broke off abruptly, a door slammed – and only the thudding of their footsteps on the stair-carpet broke the eerie silence which followed.

CHAPTER 24

Roehampton Round-up

There was no sign of Beresford in the passage.

Nor were there any signs of a struggle.

It was the sound of the slammed door which puzzled Dawlish. He stood by the foot of the staircase, looking along the passage.

'Ted had his gun in his hand, didn't he?'

'You – you know darned well he did.' Tim, more susceptible to the atmosphere than Dawlish, was breathing heavily.

'He only needed a split-second to squeeze the trigger,' said Dawlish thoughtfully, 'but instead he shouted. Odd.'

'If someone had a line on him – '

'He would have taken a chance,' said Dawlish. 'He lost his gun before he could fire, we can take that as certain. Thus: a door opened, someone either looped a rope about his gun, or took it with something working on the scissor principle. It happened quickly, so our customer wasn't unused to the job.'

'What are you talking about?' growled Tim. 'It was probably knocked out of his hand.'

'Guns, when knocked out of hands, make loud noises,' said Dawlish. 'We were seen to come in, and we were seen looking around and about. All the evidence points to the fact that anything of particular interest is belowstairs. I suppose we should really have concentrated on that part of the house before going up.'

'Where's all this talk taking us?' demanded Tim. 'We're

not in the best of spots, Pat. And where the devil *did* Ted go?'

Dawlish pursed his lips.

'We-ell, at a rough guess I'd say he either disappeared through one of the walls, or the floor. The suddenness of the trick suggests the floor.'

Tim stared at him.

'*That's* an idea. And it must have happened on the spot where Ted was standing.'

'That's why we're not standing on it,' said Dawlish drily. He raised his voice a little. 'The problem, my son, is whether to get in touch with the police.'

'Well – '

Dawlish raised a hand sharply, to stop him.

'But if we do, that cooks the case for Eileen and Black, and I've learned enough in the past twenty-four hours to believe that they're more sinned against than sinning. If we can get them clear before we put the police on to Cole, that'll suit me fine.'

Tim made a queer noise in his throat.

'Are you – '

'I'm trying to make up my mind,' said Dawlish, and muttered below his breath: 'Keep quiet, can't you? I've got another audience.' Loudly again he went on smoothly: 'Raymond Black will have to take what's coming to him for hiding his nationality, but the war won't last for ever. If we can clear him of this murder liability, it will be as much as he can expect. I'd like to know more about that murder.'

Tim fell belatedly into line.

Not until the whispered exhortation had he realised that Dawlish believed he could be heard *beneath* the floor, and even then he had not at first realised that Dawlish's chief aim was to put a completely wrong idea into Cole's mind – provided, of course, Cole was listening.

Dawlish thought he was.

He believed that Black had told him a story which, in the essentials, was fantastic. He did not think that Black's driving about the country had anything at all to do with country house burglaries. True, Black probably thought it had, but that idea could easily have been planted deliberately in his mind.

The thing of importance was to make Cole continue to believe that Dawlish's interest was unconnected with the police or the authorities. While Cole believed that, he would not run for cover but would continue whatever nefarious scheme he was planning. He would consider that Dawlish was too concerned for Black and Eileen to report to the police, and thus he, Cole, would gain valuable time.

These facts filtered dimly into Tim Jeremy's mind, and he said with feeling:

'I'd like to know about that murder too. Of all the swinish tricks – '

Dawlish said: 'I couldn't agree more, but at the moment we're concerned with getting Black and Eileen free from a murder charge. Until we do that, we can't tell the police about Cole's little games.' He paused. 'Right?'

Tim sounded reluctant.

'Ye-es, I suppose so.'

'There's no suppose about it,' said Dawlish emphatically. 'For the time being the police are out, and we'll handle this on our own.'

If Dawlish was correct, and Cole had been listening, the bait was already taken, Tim supposed, and now his anxiety about Beresford rose to the fore. 'What about finding a door to the cellar?' he suggested quietly.

'And thus doing the obvious,' answered Dawlish with a grin. 'Oh no, we're going to make a thorough search upstairs.'

'*Upstairs?*'

'Well, of course. Cole's proved himself a master of the tortuous. He engineers a hole in the floor, and through it Ted drops. That brings us down here, and makes us concentrate on the ground floor and the cellar, while Cole and his hearties are up in the attic. Remember there's a servant's staircase, and probably a continuation of it to the cellar.

Upstairs, we go, then!' He turned and Tim followed him, wanting to protest and yet uncertain whether there was a flaw in Dawlish's reasoning. It was Tim's experience that Dawlish was rarely wrong.

Dawlish started heavily up the stairs, and on the first landing stopped.

'That's far enough for me. Go up the next flight, walking normally. Come down again and don't *make a sound*.'

'Oh, my benighted Aunt!' muttered Tim Jeremy under his breath. 'What the devil *are* you trying to do?'

'I've tried to let Cole and the cellar-dwellers think we're upstairs,' whispered Dawlish. 'I fancy they'll give us five minutes, and then come out of their hiding-places below ground. They're heard us going up – let them hear your footsteps fading, and then come down, as I said.' He finished speaking and started down the stairs, treading very lightly and making no sound. The staircase was of solid oak, and not a single stair creaked. He reached the end of the passage and went along it as far as the door which communicated with the servant's quarters. There he stopped until Tim reappeared. Dawlish raised a hand, to indicate that he should stay just where he was, while he himself opened the communicating door, and then went to the end of a passage which led to a side exit from The Yews. Off the passage led pantries, a larder, and a sizeable kitchen. He slipped into the kitchen.

They waited.

The silence which had been about them before had now taken on a tension which made waiting difficult. Once or twice slight sounds made Dawlish jump, but nothing developed from them. He kept an eye on his watch, and for the second time since he had started in the hunt for Cole – and those who might be with Cole – he found time passing incredibly slowly. But the minute hand showed the passing of five minutes at last.

Almost on the instant he heard another sound.

His grip tightened about his revolver. The sound, that of a door or a panel opening, was very quiet and might not have been noticed but for the utter silence. It was followed by whispering voices.

Footsteps sounded in the passage.

They were soft and furtive, but they were unmistakable, and they were coming towards Dawlish. He made himself wait until it seemed that they were on top of him, and then he stepped into the passage, raising his voice at the same time.

'Cover that end, Tim!'

He stood squarely in the kitchen passage, the gun pushed forward; and the sight which met his eyes was almost incredible, although it was just what he wanted to see.

Cole was first; Drew was second; two other men were in their wake, each carrying a gun, each poking a gun into the ribs of another pair. Beresford, in fact, and Crummy Wise.

*

Tim, standing by the stair-head gun in hand, called in his deep voice:

'Action stations!'

Dawlish smiled, while the men in front of him stared with increasing stupefaction.

'Nice work, everything considered. I out-manoeuvred you that time, Colonel! Gentlemen – drop your guns.'

The men with the guns might have made a fight, and could at least have severely wounded Ted and Crummy. They chose to let their guns fall, for there was about Dawlish a size and grimness not easily defied.

The guns clattered to the ground.

Beresford and Crummy quickly separated, Crummy going to Tim, Beresford to Dawlish.

Dawlish said easily: 'Hallo, Ted, how did they handle you?'

Ted gulped.

'The floor opened – someone hooked my gun out of my hand, and pulled me through with a hooked stick. I hadn't an earthly. But I thought you – '

'You shouldn't think,' said Dawlish in high good humour.

'That's what Colonel Cole did, and see what a mistake he made!'

Cole drew a deep breath. The reddish-brown eyes, startled before, now narrowed. Of his two men, one half-turned, and then realised that there was no chance at all of making a fight. The other, thought Dawlish, had had all the stuffing knocked out of him with the first shock.

The only man who did not seem particularly put out was Drew. He kept a poker-face; he was, Dawlish thought, as courageous a man as he was likely to meet in this affair or any other.

It was Drew who spoke next.

'You think you're clever, Dawlish, but if you don't let us go you'll make the mistake of your life. We aren't alone, you know.'

Cole snapped: 'Shut up, Drew!'

Dawlish's interest quickened. There was nothing in his expression to suggest that he was pleased beyond words. Yet he was. Cole's snapped order was sufficient confirmation of the fact that Drew had told the truth.

There *were* others.

That was precisely what Dawlish wanted to know, and he stared at Drew and then at Cole.

'Well, well, now we're all comfortably together, suppose you talk, Drew?'

CHAPTER 25

One Confession

Cole turned towards Drew. About the Colonel there was, now, nothing pleasant, nothing of the country gentleman; he looked, in fact, only a little less villainous than the two thugs behind him.

'You keep your mouth shut, Drew!'

Drew's colour ebbed, and when Dawlish asked him again to talk more comprehensively, he kept silent. Dawlish, in fact, did not expect to get information from them at that point, and he was wondering how best to get away from the house.

Cole said repressively: 'You have been lucky this time, Dawlish. Don't push it.'

'Lucky! It was the triumph of an ingenious mind against considerable odds, and I'm quite proud of myself! However, it's time we were off. You're feeling all right, Ted?'

'I'm fine.'

'Good. You and Tim can take Drew and Cole to the flat, and I'll come along in half-an-hour. I'll look after the other thugs, with Crummy.'

Nothing more was said until Ted and Tim, with Cole and Drew, were in Tim's Bentley. The borrowed police Wolseley was standing outside the front door for Dawlish and the others. Ted Beresford sat in the tonneau with Cole, Drew sat next to Tim, who was at the wheel. Before Tim started off, Dawlish called him aside.

'Don't let them know we're lined up with the police – that's a first essential. And when you get a hundred yards or so along the road, have a spot of bother with the engine. I'll phone for a police car to pick you up at Putney Heath, and keep you in sight – it will make sure you get to the flat safely. Got all that?'

'Right!' said Tim with enthusiasm.

As the car drove off, Dawlish went into one of the rooms, in which he had seen a telephone. Lifting the receiver he spoke quickly to the Putney police. They did not delay in confirming the reliability of his instructions with the Yard, and promised to send a car to watch the Bentley; the police car was not to make itself known unless there was trouble.

Well satisfied, Dawlish returned to the kitchen, where Crummy was keeping the two thugs covered. He looked dirty, dishevelled, but extremely contented.

'Hallo, hallo!' he said, waving the gun. 'What are you going to do with these coves?'

Dawlish, rummaging in a cupboard, was lucky enough to find a length of clothes line. This served to bind the prisoners' ankles and wrists. That done, Dawlish rang the Putney police station again, and arranged for the two prisoners to be taken into custody.

Dawlish left them in a pantry until the police arrived, and, with Crummy, made a search of the house. They found nothing of importance, however. There were no papers which might be even remotely connected with the Cole organisation, and Dawlish came reluctantly to the conclusion that the house was no more than a hiding-place for the crooks, and for Cole, a convenient port of call near London.

The police arrived in twenty-five minutes.

The Inspector with them had evidently been in touch with the Yard. He was a big, plump man, and he seemed to consider the whole matter – involved as it was with an amateur detective – a great joke. But he was obliging enough, and he undertook to have the house searched so that no possible hiding-place would be overlooked.

Fully confident of this, Dawlish left him. On the way to the flat it occurred to him that although it was late afternoon, he had had no lunch. He called at a shop in Piccadilly, bought pies, fruit, and a mountain of bread-rolls, and with these returned to the flat.

He had not seriously considered the possibility that Cole and Drew could have escaped, and when he saw a police car at the end of the road he was quite sure that there was nothing to worry about. He had a word with the driver, who told him that he had followed the Bentley, and had instructions to wait for further orders from Captain Dawlish.

Dawlish showed Morely's card.

'I don't think there's anything else at the moment, thanks. You did a neat job.'

He watched the gratified driver move off, and then walked up to the flat, opening the door with a key and then going through, arms loaded with his packages.

In the lounge, Tim, Ted, Cole and Drew were waiting; the atmosphere was a long way from cordial.

Dawlish smiled about him, as if there had been nothing more than an exchange of words between friends.

'Hallo, folk, I've some viands. Hungry, Colonel?' He went through to the dining-room, and dumped the stuff on to a table. From the door he went on: 'Well, aren't we feeling talkative?'

Cole and Drew said nothing; Beresford contributed the information that they had behaved like deaf mutes all the way.

Dawlish shrugged, and suggested that Crummy should share out the food. He offered a share to Cole and Drew; it was refused, Dawlish shrugged again. As he ate and drank he thought over what had happened in the past twelve hours, and was amazed at the variety of incident, as well as at the way in which the tables had been turned.

Cole had some reason for thinking himself a victim of circumstances, while he, Dawlish, had good reason for being satisfied. But only up to a point; and that was not far enough.

He thought one thing was certain.

Cole believed that his interest was in the Blacks, and thought also that he was taking a considerable chance in risking police intervention. That was the point to stress, for he *had* to lull Cole into a sense of false security. He had to do more, but for the moment that did not matter a great deal.

Drew's words were the operative ones; but he did not think that Drew would say another word which mattered. It was certainly unlikely that the man could be frightened into talking.

Dawlish finished his scratch meal, and then went into the lounge. Only Crummy Wise showed a gun, and he sat with it in an easy chair by the door. Ted Beresford lounged near the window, and Tim stretched himself full length on a settee. He even closed his eyes; to all appearances he was asleep.

Cole and Drew remained tight-lipped, pale, and obviously worried. The behaviour of Dawlish and his friends could be reckoned to worry anyone. There was an airiness and nonchalance about it, yet these men knew that they were in danger of their lives.

Dawlish pulled a stiff-backed chair towards him, and sat astride it.

'Well, now we've had time to think,' he said.

'Dawlish – '

'Well?'

Cole drew a sharp breath. 'Why waste words,' he said.

'It's a habit of mine,' said Dawlish amiably. 'But if you prefer me to get straight to the point, all right. I don't want my leave messed up by slimy beggars of your order, you know.'

'Insults won't do you any good,' said Cole.

Dawlish said: 'You seem in danger of forgetting that it's you who are in the spot, not me.'

'You think so?'

'Have you any ideas?' asked Dawlish with interest. 'Explain them, Colonel, I'm always receptive of ideas.'

Cole took a short step forward.

'You'd better be. Dawlish, you don't seem to realise that you've made a bed of trouble for yourself. You won't find it easy to explain to the police what you've been doing – they won't take kindly to amateur interference.'

'Don't worry about me and the police,' said Dawlish. 'We're old friends. They'll forgive me when I hand them their man on a platter – particularly the man who murdered Smith.'

'You're very sure of yourself,' sneered Cole.

'Yes, that's a habit also. But I was going to get straight to the point, wasn't I?' He dropped his bantering manner. 'All right. I've heard Black's story, and Eileen Granger's. They're a couple of young fools who don't deserve to get more trouble than they've had, and if I can stop it, they won't have more trouble. Is that clear?'

Cole sneered: 'I've got them where I want them.'

'You mean, you *had*. The first cause of blackmail is no longer a strong one, you know. Black's prepared to make a full statement to the police.'

'Black killed a man – '

'Oh, no,' said Dawlish. 'Black was in a position where he could have killed a man, that's all. I'm quite sure he didn't. In fact you, or one of the little curiosities who work for you, did *that* job.'

'You're wrong. Black killed a man – and he can't prove he didn't. If you don't let me go, with Drew, I'll tell the whole story to the police. Get that fixed in your fool head, Dawlish. If you keep me here, the police will know.'

'The police would be interested to hear about you,' said Dawlish coldly.

'*I* can cover myself.'

'Really? Lucky fellow. But I don't believe you, Colonel. In fact if the Black business has to go to the police, it will only do so while you're a prisoner. Just look at the case from my point of view. I want to help that couple, and I fully intend that before I go off leave they're either going to be quite free from your filthy tricks, or you're going to be in a position where you can't do them any more harm.'

'I can do them plenty – '

'Once in jail you can only accuse them of a murder committed a year or more ago, and you can only offer proof which will in some measure incriminate yourself. But if that's got to be – all right. I'd rather see them in dock on a charge of murder, and standing a fair chance of getting a "not guilty" verdict, than I'd see them running around doing what you tell them. So, Colonel, you can take your choice. A full statement and confession of the murder of which you have accused Black. Or the police. Take which you like, but don't keep me waiting.'

Cole stared at him, and Drew took a deep breath.

'Supposing I make an admission, clearing Black?' Cole spoke tensely.

Dawlish smiled.

'I've several days of my leave left. I shall let you go. If I can't get you again for the Smith job, I'll eat my hat, but that isn't a matter for immediate discussion. The suggestion is a barter arrangement; your confession of the year-old murder, *and* also an admission that you have blackmailed Black and his girl into what other crimes they have since committed, against your freedom for a day or two. If you can make it last more than a day or two, I won't complain. My interest is strictly on behalf of the couple you've treated so damnably. Am I understood?'

Crummy Wise leaned forward in his chair.

'I say, Pat, that's a bit hot!'

'Let him alone,' said Ted Beresford. 'He always was a crazy fool.'

Cole said like a man in a dream:

'Can I *rely* on your word?'

Dawlish smiled. 'Try it, and see. It's the police for certain if you don't make this confession.'

Cole said sharply: 'Give me some paper.' He stepped to the small bureau in the room, and when Dawlish gave him paper and pen, he wrote swiftly for several minutes. When he had finished Dawlish read through a comprehensive statement which sufficiently covered the Black-Eileen angle. Cole watched him reading, and when that was finished said slowly:

'Now it's up to you to keep your part of the bargain, Dawlish.'

CHAPTER 26

Dawlish Decides

Dawlish stepped back from the table and re-read the statement. It implicated Cole and Drew, and there was no doubt that in the hands of the police it would be enough to send Cole to the gallows. In short, Cole had signed an admission to complicity in a year-old murder case, and one which would be damning in a court of law.

He had done it on the chance of getting free.

He had done it knowing that Dawlish might refuse to carry out his share of the bargain; he had, in fact, taken a chance that was no more than evens – and few men would have considered it evens. One thing was quite clear; it showed the degree of importance which Cole put on getting away for a few hours.

Drew was watching the large man, narrow-eyed.

Cole snapped: 'Well, what about it?'

'Hard though you'll find it to believe, I'm going to keep my word,' said Dawlish. 'I'm going to let you go, Cole – but I'm coming after you again.'

'That's not – '

'I implied that I would do so before you signed the statement,' said Dawlish. 'I'm going to give you precisely twelve hours of freedom. And then I'm coming after you. You see, Colonel, there are other things I want to know. The police might get you for this murder, but on the other hand you could swear that you made the confession under duress – threats of violence, for instance. Oh, I'm not blind to the implications, so I'll give you just twelve hours before I take up the trail.'

Cole said: 'You'll be wise to keep out of it.'

'Probably you are right. Unfortunately I was always inclined to like a spree,' said Dawlish. He stepped to a chair where Cole's hat was resting and picked it up. He handed it to Cole, bowed slightly, and pointed to the door. 'Good-day, Colonel.'

Cole started to his feet.

'What about Drew?'

'We made no conditions about Drew,' said Dawlish amiably. 'He stays.'

'But – '

'If you're going to argue any more about it, the deal's off,' said Dawlish sharply. 'I'm not all of a fool, Cole. I can use Drew, and you'd find him invaluable, I haven't any doubt of that. So I'll make the use of him, and you'll manage on your own, as best you can. You, and the friends Drew talked about.'

Cole looked sharply at his colleague.

'You keep your mouth shut,' he said, and then stepped across the room. Crummy made no effort to stop him. Cole hesitated, as if he could not believe this was really happening. Crummy stretched up a hand, with some effort, and opened the door.

Cole went through.

Ted Beresford stood up from the window as the door closed, and said quickly:

'Who follows him?'

'None of us,' said Dawlish. 'A bargain's a bargain, and the Colonel has twelve hours to clear out. On the whole,' he added thoughtfully, 'the only man with a justifiable complaint is Drew. Eh, Drew?'

The man looked at him coldly.

'If you think I'm a talker, you're wrong.'

Dawlish shrugged.

'Oh, I'm quite sure about that. I've nothing against your pluck. I'm going to turn you over to the police *pronto* and they can work on you in their own sweet way.'

Drew started.

'The police – '

Dawlish drawled:

'My dear man, have I succeeded in deceiving even you? I'm working *with* the police. They know all about Cole's part in the robberies, or what-have-you. They're watching the gentleman very carefully indeed – why should I do their job for them just now?'

'You – the police – '

'Yes. I've taken Prior's place,' said Dawlish. 'Surprising, isn't it?'

'But – ' Drew had lost every vestige of colour, and his eyes were blank. 'But the Blacks – '

'A very interesting angle with which we've been able to make a deal,' said Dawlish. 'I'll worry about the Blacks later. I won't worry about you at all, the police can do that.' He stepped to the telephone, and dialled Whitehall 1212. He spoke to Morely, and arranged for Drew to be collected. Throughout the time he was on the telephone Drew was staring at him incredulously.

Dawlish replaced the receiver, and said:

'That's that. One act over, Drew. I'm almost sorry for you.' He flicked the ash off his cigarette, and then said clearly: 'How much does Berlin pay you?'

Drew stared.

'B-Berlin?'

'Yes, you heard me.'

'What – what are you talking about?' muttered Drew. 'You must be mad, there's no connection with Berlin, there's nothing but – but the robberies Cole's staged. Black told you all about them – '

'Oh yes, he told me all about them, but I didn't believe it.'

'But it's true!' Drew screeched, and for the first time he lost his composure. 'It's absolutely true, that's all there is in it! Cole's organised a series of robberies – '

'Tell it to the marines,' said Dawlish brusquely. 'Cole's organising a mass attack on agriculture – my sainted aunt, did you really think that we were as innocent as that? Do

162

you really think I let Cole go to give him a chance? My dear fellow, I let him go so that he can contact the other agents. I let him go because he's clearly a pawn, and I want the kingpin. I let him go because he's far more use outside than he is inside.'

'I – I can't believe it,' muttered Drew, his face suddenly haggard. 'Not *you*, Dawlish, you're too much of a fool, you – '

'You think so? Well, better men than you have done that,' said Dawlish easily. 'Supposing you tell me who killed Smith? Was it Cole?'

Drew nodded.

'Who poisoned Prior?'

'I don't know.'

'I suppose I can't expect you to talk much,' said Dawlish. 'But tell me, are you English?'

Drew's tongue ran along his lips.

'Please don't say anything as trite as that you're English and proud of it,' begged Dawlish.

'English! – *Gott in himmel!*' Drew was sweating freely, his breath coming in uneven gasps. 'What can I make of the English, never the same, never what you expect. You – Dawlish – ' he choked. 'I'm no more English than Black is, I'll live to see you crushed, all of you and your rotten country, I'll – '

'I think that's enough,' said Dawlish evenly.

'More than enough,' said Ted Beresford.

'Excessively so,' said Crummy Wise.

They all gazed coldly, indifferently, at Drew.

They saw a different man. The resistance, mental more than physical, had gone from him, and he looked back dazedly from one man to another. The flat was silent for some seconds, and then Dawlish shrugged.

'Oh, well. That's one quisling less in this country. What do they do with quislings?'

'In this country, shoot 'em I hope,' said Tim.

It was not long before the police arrived. When Drew had gone, Dawlish stood by the door and looked down at the others, all of whom had taken up positions of comfort and ease about the lounge.

'Well?' he said.

'Well,' said Tim after a pause, 'I think you're quite mad. You've always been on the border-line, but after this show-down I don't need a doctor to certify you. Why, in heaven's name, did you let Cole go? If I could see any sense in it I wouldn't complain, but I can't see a ha'porth.'

'I'm with Tim,' announced Ted Beresford firmly.

'I can't make head or tail of it,' declared Crummy Wise, 'but I suppose you know what you're doing, Pat. Did I tell you what happened to me, by the way?'

Nobody answered him, but Crummy didn't need an answer.

Enthusiastically he launched into his story. 'Well, I kept on Cole's tail for an hour or more, and arrived at Putney Heath. There he went into a pub. I was just cogitating whether to follow him or stay where I was, when along came a small car, and guess what! Out stepped one of the thugs. He threatened me with a gun and ordered me to get into the car; an order which, under the circumstances, I meekly obeyed. Then we weighed anchor at the Roehampton house, and I didn't know any more about it until Ted arrived. Afterwards – you came along, and we heard you jabbering. I can't tell you how almighty glad I was, and so,' went on Crummy with feeling, 'I propose to give you the benefit of the doubt until you're proved insane. All the same – why did you let him go?'

Dawlish grinned. 'Because, you ass, I think he will go hell-for-leather to his home. It's watched. I think he'll get in touch with the top rank plotters. We want them badly. *What the devil's that?*'

'That' was a crash outside followed by a sharp staccato noise which came from not far away. It was familiar; Dawlish knew the sound of a tommy-gun when he heard it, and his question was automatic, rather than one requiring an answer. He stepped to the window and looked into the street; at one end he saw a small crowd crouching behind some parked cars. Further ahead, he saw a car from which the snout of a tommy-gun was poking, and he saw the flashes of flame coming from it.

'Come on,' he said.

All four reached the street in less than thirty seconds. Then it was that they saw a car on its side, explaining the crash. They also saw Drew, on his feet and running.

From the smaller car the machine-gun bullets sprayed the sides of the street, giving Drew clearance.

Suddenly Dawlish cried: '*Down!*'

They hardly needed telling what to do, and as they dropped to ground level the direction of the shooting altered, and the bullets came dangerously near.

CHAPTER 27

Desperation

There was a peculiar sense of satisfaction in Dawlish's mind as he reached the pavement. He had time to draw his revolver, and he did not think any of the others would have been slow in doing the same. The duel would not be long, for the car was in a far more vulnerable position than any of the prostrate men.

That was not the cause of his satisfaction.

It was the very violence of the attempt to save Drew which pleased him, for in that violence he read at last, desperation. He had played, first to last, with that objective in view, but the calmness had been an unnerving and a disquieting thing, for calmness suggested confidence, and he had not liked to think that the men working with Cole were so sure of themselves.

This open war-fare was proof that they were not.

It also suggested that Drew held a key position, and that was another reason for not letting him go.

All those things passed through Dawlish's mind as he fell, and drew his gun. The *tap-tap-tap* of the tommy-gun merged with the dull thudding of bullets in the walls of the houses alongside, and chips of granite flew about them. Then added to that noise was the roar of revolver shooting. The four of them fired almost simultaneously, and the bullets crashed from four directions towards the front of the smaller car.

Abruptly, the tommy-gun stopped.

As abruptly the car turned towards the kerb, the driver slumped across his wheel. The machine-gunner was not in sight, and the snout of his weapon had disappeared.

Drew managed to get clear.

Dawlish hauled himself to his feet, and began to run in his wake. The man was showing a turn of speed that surprised him. Many things were surprising about Drew. Dawlish was not surprised, however, when Drew half-turned and, for the first time, showed a gun.

The bullet flew wide.

Dawlish went on running. He wanted a prisoner, not a corpse. He hoped that he would get one, but at the back of his mind there was the fear that Drew might shoot himself. He redoubled his efforts as they neared a corner, and then he saw that Drew would get a considerable advantage if he once made the turning.

So Dawlish fired, very low.

People had scattered in all directions, their frightened faces peering from behind cover at the two men. A policeman ran from the far end of Brook Street, aiming to cut Drew off. Drew fired at him, and the man pulled up, then fell slowly forward.

Dawlish fired again.

Drew had now reached the corner. Dawlish saw him stagger, and then saw him plunge forward. By then, another policeman was running up, and he reached the escaping man before Dawlish. When Dawlish reached them Drew was rolling over and over with the policeman, biting and kicking, punching and gouging, in a fight which conformed to no rules, but showing a physical courage far beyond the average.

Dawlish reached them, and half regretfully cracked the butt of his gun against Drew's temple. The blow was not hard enough to do serious damage, but was nicely calculated to put the man out. It succeeded, and the policeman, cheeks scratched and bleeding and knuckles grazed, climbed unsteadily to his feet.

'Th-thank you, sir.'

'Always glad to be of service,' said Dawlish, breathing a little heavily. 'And we wanted that gentleman very badly. How are you?'

'I'll be all right in a minute or two, sir.'

'Good,' said Dawlish. 'If you feel anything like me, a mouthful of this won't hurt you.' He took a whisky-flask from his hip-pocket, handing it to the man, who drank gratefully. Dawlish followed his example, and when he lowered the flask Tim's sepulchral voice sounded just behind him.

'What a time to drink a toast!'

'All times are whisky times,' said Dawlish lightly, and offered the flask to Tim, who refused.

He smiled fleetingly. 'Is he right out?'

'Only temporarily,' said Dawlish. 'He'll wake up in hospital.' He straightened up, and by then other police had arrived, and there was a welter of explanations. Dawlish learned with relief that there had been no serious injury to any civilians; the one casualty who would need hospital treatment was the plucky constable who had run towards Drew despite the gun; he was likely to be on the danger list for some time.

The quartette was back at the flat half-an-hour after leaving it; the actual fracas had started and finished in a little more than ten minutes. All of them felt weary, but only Tim was tired out. On Dawlish's suggestion he went to bed. He had not slept a wink the night before, because of the chase after Black.

Thinking of this, Dawlish pulled up sharply.

'Now what's the matter?' Ted demanded.

'Not another idea!' groaned Crummy Wise.

With a strained expression on his face, Dawlish stepped to the bathroom, the spare bedroom, and then the dining-room. The others watched him, until he had finished. Then he faced them again, and said in an odd voice:

'Who was it said I was crazy?'

'I contributed,' said Ted.

'You were quite right.'

'What the devil *are* you talking about?' demanded Crummy Wise. 'What do you think's hidden in the rooms? A tarantula or a boa-constrictor, or something?'

Dawlish said evenly:

'I don't think anything or anyone's hidden in the flat. I wish they were. It's not your worry, Crummy, you knew nothing about it. But I've had my mind so full of other things that I forgot who we left at the flat. I *forgot* it. Black and Stenner were here, Black, and Stenner! And a police car was supposed to be on guard.'

*

From the moment they had returned to the flat to the moment when Dawlish remembered Raymond Black, there had not been an idle moment. Or so the others tried to persuade Dawlish, but he was not easily persuaded. He had had time to telephone the police while Cole and Drew had been at the flat; he had neglected the opportunity and lost well over an hour.

He could not get over it. How *could* he have forgotten the man in the space of an hour or two?

It had happened, and a little later he went as far as to grudgingly admit that there was a certain amount of excuse for it. The rush of events, the spell at Roehampton, and the fact that Black had been left on his own and not under guard, all contributed to the ease with which he had been forgotten.

In haste Dawlish telephoned Morely, and learnt that there had been no report from the policemen in the car watching the flat.

'The instructions were clear enough,' Dawlish said. 'They were to stop anyone getting in or going out. Two men did go out.'

'They'll have followed your men,' said Morely a little uncertainly.

'Now, Archie! If I'd employed some amateurs they might have taken it into their heads to do a job of work without asking for orders, but your men wouldn't go against definite instructions, and you know it as well as I do.'

Morely grunted.

'So it means that your men, Black and the little cove

have been spirited away,' said Dawlish slowly. 'Oh, well – we'll just keep searching. Have you had any more news?'

'One small item,' Morely told him. 'I've had a medical report on the drug which affected Prior. It was an irritant poison, affecting the throat more than the stomach. The doctor down there did a good job, according to the specialists.'

'He seemed capable enough,' admitted Dawlish. 'I suppose Prior isn't able to talk?'

'No, and I don't think he could tell us much if he could.'

'You don't sound too happy, what's the trouble?' asked Dawlish.

There was silence for a moment, and then Morely said: 'I'm worried. We're all worried – but there's been no new development, except one or two serious outbreaks of foot-and-mouth, and one or two more fires with stacked corn.'

Dawlish said sharply: 'Where?'

'In Hampshire – '

'What part? I – just a minute, Archie. I've been wool-gathering – '

'Is *that* what it is,' said Morely tartly. 'I thought you'd been gathering specimens. We've got five or six at Canonn Row, but not one of them will say a helpful word. I've also been making discreet inquiries about Colonel Cole. I think you've made a blunder there, and I don't advise you to act without talking to me first. He's reputable in every way.'

'Oh, my Lord!' exclaimed Dawlish. 'He's about as reputable as a rattlesnake. He's in this up to the neck, and in my pocket I've a signed confession that he was one of three men who committed a murder at the Old Swan Inn, near Winchester, about eleven months ago. I've let him go haring back to the Lodge. He's well-looked after there, and I'm going down myself in an hour or so. He'll have to contact with others of his precious gang, and it's the rest we want as well as Cole himself. Now listen, Archie, as soon as you can, let me have a marked map of the country in which the fires and the foot-and-mouth trouble have occurred. And send out a call for the car-load of men who were watching the flat.

Try to find 'em – I must get Black back, it's the nearest thing to essential that I know. I – and Archie! Telephone Winchester, and ask them to have a cordon of men thrown about Marsham Lodge. Yes, *Marsham*, where I've been staying.'

'What is all this about?' Morely was startled. 'Have you gone mad?'

'That's the second time today I've been asked that. But no, I haven't,' said Dawlish. 'You can take Cole's complicity as gospel truth, and with a little luck I'll have the rest of it in a matter of twelve hours, so leave it to me – '

'You want the Lodge watched but nothing done?' Morely's voice was understandably faint.

'No one is to come out – any one who wants to can go in,' said Dawlish. 'And I'm particularly worried about Eileen Granger. Have you got all that?' Dawlish brushed his hair back from his forehead which was damp with perspiration.

'Yes, but – '

'I'm on my way to the Lodge,' said Dawlish more calmly. 'I'll 'phone you again from there, old man. Forgive the excitement but new ideas have suddenly occurred to me.'

'I don't mind your excitement, provided the new ideas are not caused by delusions,' said Morely. 'Can't you give me a hint of what it's all about?'

'Yes,' said Dawlish. 'Black is the important factor. Black did not necessarily leave here of his own accord – he could have been abducted. He can close our case for us, and so can Eileen. He's gone, she's in danger, and I don't want her to be hurt. For that matter – ' he paused for some seconds, then went on thoughtfully: 'It might be an idea if you told Winchester to arrest her. Will you see to it?'

'But you just said – '

'She's in acute danger,' said Dawlish emphatically, 'but in Winchester police-station she should be fairly safe. Will you do that?'

CHAPTER 28

Haste to the Lodge

He would have understood it had Morely insisted on knowing more. He realised, when he was calmer, that he had let himself think aloud, an even more confusing business over the telephone than in normal conversation. He was quite sure that he was right; and he hoped against hope that he could convince Morely of the need for acting on his suggestions.

Morely said quietly:

'All right, Pat, I'll look after her.'

A great wave of relief swept over Dawlish. 'Thanks,' he said. 'I'll ring you again just as soon as I can.' He replaced the telephone, and looked across at Ted. 'Oh, damn,' he said mildly. 'I forgot to tell Archie that Drew must be held at all costs. Ring him for me, will you – suggest that they put guards by the door and the window of Drew's room, whereever he is.'

Beresford took the receiver, and dialled Whitehall again, while Dawlish went into the bathroom and ran ice-cold water over his face and eyes. He felt fresher when he rejoined the others.

'You've gathered the gist of what I've been saying, I hope.'

'We-ell – ' said Ted, Tim and Crummy, in unison.

'Apparently you haven't. We'll talk about it on the way down. We'll all go in the Bentley, Tim – how is it for petrol?'

'Nearly full.'

'Good.' Dawlish led the way downstairs, and when they had settled into the car, he took the wheel, and began to talk.

'We'll work it out together as far as I've gone,' he said. 'Black and Eileen, blackmailed into doing what they're told, drive other people from place to place about the countryside. They're told it's a series of robberies. Right?'

'Right,' said Ted, next to him.

'Good. Actually, the robberies are imaginary. Black and Eileen have played no part in that kind of crime. Now look at the other side of the problem, Archie's side, and Prior's. They have been worried by a great deal of trouble in the very same part of the country as that in which the supposed robberies have occurred. Fires, poisoned seeds, and above all foot-and-mouth disease. Now foot-and-mouth disease is contagious. To prevent it spreading, therefore, the authorities close down certain areas, to stop cattle carrying the disease from one field to another. Right?'

Murmurs of assent, varying in degree, answered him.

Dawlish slid the Bentley between a lorry and a bus with hardly an inch to spare on either side. 'Well, if the movement of cattle would spread the disease, presumably the movements of a part of one would also do it. The bodies of the affected beasts are buried these days, because of the blackout. It wouldn't be impossible for two or three men to go to an affected area, disinter some part of an affected carcass, and take it to another, unaffected part of the country.'

'Good – good Gad!'

'What an idea!'

'Oh, crumbs!' came from Dawlish's three listeners.

'Precisely,' said Dawlish drily. 'Supposing – and I think we can suppose it – Black has been driving men from place to place and spreading the foot-and-mouth disease? It would explain a lot – the suit-cases for instance. One suit-case loaded with the germs pushed into a cow-byre *by night*. Or dumped into a drinking trough. It speaks for itself, doesn't it?'

Clearly the others thought that it did.

There was silence for some time. Indeed, it was not until they were on the Great West Road that Tim Jeremy said slowly:

'There's one thing, Pat.'

'Hm-hm?'

'What about the fires? If they were started at night they would be seen pretty quickly. And –'

'And what?' asked Dawlish, glancing over his shoulder. 'It's a point, Tim, but not a big one. Delayed-action incendiary leaflets, like the things we've showered on Germany, would do the trick. And slow-acting poison would affect seed stores. Oh, it could all be done very easily and neatly. The thing that Cole's had to make sure of, is that no one who really mattered in his organisation was suspect. That's where Black came in. He was a ready made victim. He didn't know who he was driving about, and if he did think of giving Cole away, there was always the threat of being suspected of murder, hanging over him. Oh Cole could rely on Black keeping silent, and of course as soon as there seemed any real danger, Black would be bumped off.'

'Ye-es,' said Ted Beresford. 'But why wasn't he bumped off instead of Smith? Cole must have realised someone was watching him – watching Black, I mean.'

'Smith was expendable to Cole, Black was not. Cole was using him at the Lodge, and as a means of handling me.' Dawlish smiled a little grimly. 'One way and the other it's been a waggon-load of complications, but it's working out.'

'You think they took Black away?'

'I do – and I wish to heaven I'd not missed that angle at the first. Black could, of course, be really working *with* Cole, but I don't think so. It's much more likely that Stenner regained consciousness, and that the flat had been watched by his gang and an entrance forced before the police could stop it. The police would go up to the flat to find what was what, and walk into a trap something like we did when we first caught Drew. What happened to the police then is a different matter. I hope they're all right, but –'

'It's what has happened to Black that's worrying you.'

'You've said it,' said Dawlish, lapsing into a cliche. 'Also, what might happen to Eileen. I hope Morely's not too late. I hope –' he stopped, and shrugged his shoulders.

'You're taking it pretty well for granted that Cole went back to his house.'

'He has to keep papers and documents somewhere, and he has to keep a store of delayed-action incendiaries, or whatever he uses for the fires. And – there's someone else behind him. Drew let it out, Cole confirmed it.'

'Any idea who?' asked Ted.

But Dawlish would neither confirm nor deny such a notion.

As he had outlined the scheme, its execution was simple. It could be done; surely it had been done? All four of them thought so, but three wondered whether Dawlish was right in taking it for granted that Cole would return to his own house. They were all of them careful, keeping their eyes on the road behind them, and at the narrow turns and at crossroads Dawlish drove with extra care. But there was nothing at all to suggest that they were being followed, or that there was any watch on the road for them.

In a little under an hour and three-quarters, they reached Ringwood.

Dawlish did not stop in the small market town, although he smiled to himself when he saw *Betty's Tea Shop*. He thought of the charming old lady who had persuaded Felicity to have coffee, and he marvelled that it had happened only the day before.

He remembered the little Cockney soldier who had given the woman at the shop the lie, and had afterwards come in at the window at just the right time. He thought of everything that had happened at the Lodge, of Prior's illness, of Millsham's quick and effective treatment. He ran through the apparent contradictions in Raymond Black. He was reasonably sure that Black in his last story had told the truth, yet at the back of his mind there was a fear that the man was making a fool of him.

If that were so, then Drew and Cole had supported it cleverly – too cleverly, Dawlish thought. He smiled to himself, for in having Eileen Granger arrested he would cause something of a sensation at the Lodge, and if he allowed any suspicions about her, then he was sabotaging his own case.

He felt fairly sure that he was on the right line.

What he did not yet know was the extent to which the plot was planned, and the identity of all who were engaged in it. But there were theories in his mind, some only half-formed, which would certainly have surprised the others. They concerned Drew, and Drew's amazing change of manner.

The desperate effort to free Drew was another thing of interest.

Why was Drew so important?

Wondering about this, but not allowing himself to jump to any heady conclusion Dawlish drove along the road from Ringwood to Marsham Lodge. He passed a patrol of Home Guards, and, nearer the Lodge grounds, one or two plain-clothes men. When, finally, he pulled into the drive he found the gates shut, and three men standing in front of them. He recognised a sergeant who had worked with Woodley, and he was allowed to go through without further hindrance.

He saw Woodley on the steps.

As he pulled up he saw Pierpont and Millsham also, and one of the women who had acted as stretcher-bearer to Prior. That there had been a further accident or illness was fairly apparent, and a fear flashed through his mind that it might affect Felicity. He was halfway out of the car when that fear disappeared, for from the far side of the house Felicity came running.

Dawlish hurried to meet her, seeing the strain at her eyes, and the unusual pallor of her cheeks. She gripped his hands as he extended them.

'Hallo, darling! What's the excitement?'

She paused, drew a deep breath, and then said quickly:

'Seeing you, I think! I've been worried stiff about you – it didn't seem possible you'd come through this time. Pat, they've arrested Eileen.'

A second wave of relief went through him.

'A precautionary measure, only, darling. I told them to.'

176

'You – ' she stopped short, and shrugged her slim shoulders. 'Well, thank heavens you did! A maid was in her room just after she'd gone. Someone shot her – the whole place was in uproar. It – it was Frederick's wife.'

Dawlish thought of Frederick the porter-gardener, the continual grumbler, who had been prevented from returning to London by a wife who longed for the 'safety' of the country. The irony of this passed Dawlish by for the moment, while Felicity went on:

'It was Frederick who shot her. He thought it was Eileen. When he found what he'd done he shot himself.'

CHAPTER 29

Tragedy of Frederick

That was the bare outline.

An hour later he had the story in greater detail from Woodley and Pierpont. Frederick had been on duty in the Lodge at the time Eileen had been arrested and taken away. She had been charged in the grounds, and there had been no knowledge of her arrest inside. Then had come a shot on the first floor, and Pierpont, close at hand, had hurried to the 'Blacks' room and found the maid dead from a wound in the back of the head.

Frederick had been belowstairs when he had been told who had died.

Immediately – and there was the evidence of three maids to support that – he had stood up, and walked into the grounds. He had been seen going through the shrubbery, and then had been lost to sight. There had been the sound of another shot, and Frederick's voice raised as if in frenzy.

'*I killed her, I killed her!*'

A second shot; and then silence.

When the police on duty had reached him, he was dead, the revolver in his hand. Woodley had a working theory; and it seemed that there was no other to fit the facts.

Frederick, obviously, had received orders to kill Eileen Granger, and had seen a woman sitting at her dressing-table. A shot through a narrowly opened door had been all that was necessary. To find he had murdered his own wife in mistake for Eileen had been too much for him, and he had committed suicide.

Woodley was grave-faced.

'I don't think there's anything else we can assume, Captain Dawlish. It's a grim business, but at least Mrs Black is safe.'

'Mrs Black? Oh, oh yes.' Dawlish rubbed a hand over his hair. 'She's in Winchester, is she?'

'Yes, well-looked after. I understood from London that it was – er – detentive arrest.'

'You haven't seen Black himself?'

'Not since yesterday, no.'

'I suppose not,' said Dawlish a little vaguely. 'So Frederick had orders to kill Mrs Black, did he? The inference is that someone near here gave the orders – he'd hardly receive them by telephone.'

'No,' said Woodley.

'Frederick could easily have worked the trick with Prior's aspirins,' said Dawlish slowly. 'And he could have slipped the message under my door. Poor beggar.'

Woodley raised his eyebrows.

'I don't feel particularly sorry for him.'

'Don't you?' said Dawlish sharply. 'Then you must forgive me if I do. You see, I knew Frederick fairly well – we were acquaintances for years in London, and I don't believe he had anything to do with the killing. I do believe he knew something about the other business, and I think he knew who did do the shooting. What would be more natural, if he knew that, than for him to take a gun and go to find the man who had shot his wife? And what more sensible than for the murderer to watch for him, shoot him, cry in a strained voice – an unrecognisable kind of voice, mind you: "I killed her, I killed her!", fire another shot in the air, and then make off? Frederick was thus presented as a ready-made murderer; his suicide and shouted words serving as a confession of guilt.'

Woodley said sharply:

'It's a fantastic theory, and far less likely to be true than the obvious one.'

'The whole thing is fantastic,' admitted Dawlish. 'The most fantastic thing of all is that Frederick should be credited with shooting any woman, or any man, for that matter.' He saw Woodley's set face, and smiled a little. 'Sorry, old man. I'm jumping too fast, I know – I haven't the habit of careful thinking, it's a police quality. But if the bullet which killed Mrs Frederick and that which killed the porter came from the same gun, I'll be surprised.'

'The calibre of the bullets was the same.'

'If you'll get it checked up, I'll appreciate it,' said Dawlish.

Woodley, still affronted, said stiffly that he would have it checked. The subsequent report came in quickly, a ballistics expert in Winchester giving it as his opinion that the bullet which had killed the maid was fired from a different gun from that which had killed Frederick. Woodley telephoned this news at once to Dawlish.

'It strengthens your opinion, Captain Dawlish – '

'Ye-es,' said Dawlish. 'And it was a lucky break for us, Inspector, for whoever killed Fred could easily have stolen his gun first, and the ballistics expert would have "proved" me wrong.'

'You see what it implies,' said Woodley.

'I see part of it, yes,' admitted Dawlish. 'There's someone else in or about the Lodge. You've still got the place surrounded, as the Yard suggested?'

'Yes – no one will get out.'

'Good man,' said Dawlish. He smiled at Felicity, who was standing near him. Ted, Tim and Crummy, had gone on to Cole's house, after Dawlish had learned that Lockwood and his off-duty men were in the neighbourhood, and that some members of the Home Guard were maintaining their 'manoeuvres'. That his suggestions should have been adopted so promptly was more than gratifying; Dawlish was to learn afterwards that special word had been sent to the Regional Home Guard commander to co-operate, while Lockwood, through his C.O., had been told to assist Dawlish wherever possible.

Now, Dawlish turned again to the telephone.

'What else did the Yard say?'

'That you had *carte blanche*,' Woodley told him promptly. 'I don't quite know what it's about yet, but – '

'Careful,' warned Dawlish. 'Seeing that there's someone at the Lodge who could be implicated, the line could be tapped.'

'Do you seriously think so?'

'Very seriously,' said Dawlish. 'Now I'm going to look about the grounds where Smith was killed, Inspector.' He spoke more formally and, Felicity suspected, for the benefit of anyone who might be listening-in.

'I'll be at the office most of the night,' Woodley promised.

Dawlish replaced the receiver, and put his arm round Felicity. 'It's not much good telling you I'm sorry, is it?'

'Not a bit,' said Felicity, giving him a friendly peck on the nose. 'I used to think I'd get accustomed to you going off on one of these jaunts, but I never do, and now I know I never will.' She ruffled his hair. 'What's next?'

'I'm going to Ley Manor, for a word with Lockwood. *If* Cole's there it's time I acted. If he isn't, I may have made the biggest bloomer in my young life. I think – ' he paused again, and then nodded as if in answer to a question he had put to himself. 'I think I'll have a look at the shrubbery, for effect. You watch the house, and tell me if anyone seems to be prowling about unnecessarily. Before I go I'll send word to Ley Manor, for news, or otherwise, of Cole.'

'Won't one of the others come back with it?'

'I told 'em to wait for me,' said Dawlish.

The knowledge that in everything he did at the Lodge, he might be privately observed, was very hampering. It was possible that a servant was watching, equally possible that one of the guests was concerned. There was, in fact, no one in whom he could repose implicit confidence, except the police and his close friends. Consequently when he reached the grounds he stopped by a uniformed policeman and appeared to do no more than pass the time of the day. Actually:

'Have word sent to Ley Manor, constable – not the Manor itself, the guards – '

'I understand, sir.'

'Good man. Ask whether Colonel Cole has returned, and tell one of my friends – you know them?'

'Yes, sir.'

'To bring word back to me. Is that clear?'

Footsteps sounded near them, and Dawlish's voice went on with never a pause after his last words – 'a great pity, constable, they won't get another man as good as Frederick easily. Men are hard enough to get at all these days.'

'Very true, sir.'

The constable walked steadily on, and Dawlish turned, to find Dr Millsham not five yards away from him. Millsham smiled his somewhat portentous smile.

'I thought I'd better not interrupt, Captain Dawlish, but I would like a word with you.'

'Certainly. I'm at your service.'

The doctor's smile had disappeared. 'I wondered if you had any further news of Mr Prior? I've made inquiries, but absolute secrecy seems to surround his condition.'

'They call it red-tape,' said Dawlish, with a shrug. 'Yes, he's doing fine – in fact I was told in London yesterday that you did a very good job on him indeed. It was an irritant poison – '

Millsham looked gratified.

'That's pleasing, very pleasing. Well, I'm extremely glad that Prior is likely to recover. Whether our friend Pierpont will, is another matter, I'm afraid.'

Dawlish stared.

'Pierpont? He's all right, isn't he?'

'Bodily, yes. Mentally – ' Millsham frowned. 'He's a very worried man; and quite naturally so. The police won't let anyone leave the Lodge at the moment, but several of the people who have lived here since the hotel was opened have their bags packed and are ready to leave as soon as the ban is lifted. Pierpont lost a great deal when he was bombed out in London, and he put all his capital in Marsham Lodge.'

'Oh,' said Dawlish slowly. 'That's bad.'

'I'm glad you see it that way. I don't really know what you can do,' added Millsham a little awkwardly, 'but if there is anything – such as getting the business settled quickly, and making it clear quite to the residents that the danger had been only temporary, Pierpont would be grateful.'

'It won't last a day longer than I can help,' said Dawlish. 'But I've no idea how long that will be. It's in the early stages, I'm afraid.'

Millsham's face dropped.

'I had hoped – ' he shrugged. 'It can't be helped, of course, but it is most distressing. Pierpont strove so hard to make it a safe rendezvous for his old patrons.'

'Those who run out on him now aren't worth keeping,' said Dawlish.

'Their money is, unfortunately,' said Millsham. 'Well, I've put in my oar rather too freely, I'm afraid. I'm sure you'll understand my motives – '

'Perfectly,' said Dawlish gravely. 'And it's extremely good of you. I'll have a word with Pierpont myself a little later.'

Dawlish, watching the doctor's retreating back, thought: He's not altogether disinterested – I wonder if he works on a commission basis, or gets a regular salary? He walked on into the shrubbery, where he stayed for twenty minutes, turning the affair over in his mind, and watching all the time for the slightest suggestion of anything out of the ordinary.

But there was no movement beyond that made by two or three plainclothes men. He saw them, and examined their card and then told himself somewhat grimly that anyone who tried tricks in the grounds of Marsham Lodge was asking for trouble. Woodley had done his job well; the place was properly sealed up. And, thought Dawlish, it would remain so for a matter of hours, if not days. He had been anxious first for the safety of Eileen; now that he knew the Lodge harboured a spy, or spies, from the Cole organisation, it had become as important as Ley Manor.

He reached the Lodge again less than an hour after he had started from it. Felicity was sitting in a deck-chair in the porch. She said quietly:

'Only Millsham went after you, Pat. No one else walked towards the shrubbery at all.'

Dawlish smiled. 'He's getting anxious, and tells me that Pierpont is, as well. That can't be helped. I – hallo, here come the lads.'

Actually Crummy was coming up the drive in the Bentley, and with him was Lockwood. They drew up, and Dawlish stepped towards them the easier to hear Crummy's dispirited words:

'You backed a loser this time, Pat. Cole's not returned.'

CHAPTER 30

A Loser?

Dawlish stood back from the car as the others climbed out. No one else was nearby, and they could talk with reasonable safety. Lockwood told him that there was no way in which entry could have been forced to the grounds of Ley Manor, while the house itself was being watched from a point of vantage inside the grounds. No one had visited the place at all.

'Tim and Ted are staying around until they hear from you,' said Crummy. 'Is it any use them staying?'

'Yes, definitely,' said Dawlish, tersely. 'Obviously the man won't come back until after dark.'

Crummy raised his eyebrows.

'D'you know, I hadn't thought of that.'

'It didn't occur to me, either,' admitted Lockwood ruefully.

'You've arranged for the guard all night?'

'Yes, of course.'

Dawlish frowned in concentration. 'Of course, Cole could have been warned that the place is watched. And if anyone of the Cole mob is keeping watch, they'll know that all right. So the probability is that Cole will wait for a relaxation of the watch.'

'He could go somewhere else,' Crummy said gloomily. 'As a matter of fact, that's probably what he *will* do.'

'It's the obvious thing,' said Lockwood.

'The desperate thing,' said Dawlish, 'for it presumes that he's quite prepared to give up his position in the county, and to make himself what the police records would call a fugitive from justice.' He looked at his watch. 'It's half-past seven. Dinner's late. I wish,' he added as he turned into the Lodge, 'that it grew dark a couple of hours earlier. As soon as it *is* dark, – about half-past nine, I suppose – I'm going into Winchester to see Eileen. Coming Felicity?'

'What about me?' demanded Crummy.

'Take over from one of the others at the Manor when you've had dinner,' said Dawlish. 'One of us should be around there all the time. And as for staying *here* – every confounded movement watched, every – ' He stopped. 'But I'm getting morbid.'

The dinner-gong rang then, and Dawlish, Crummy, Lockwood and Felicity dined together at the same table. Pierpont, superintending as usual, had nothing of his usual evening-smile, and when he reached their table Dawlish saw that his plump face was pale, and his eyes looked worried. Millsham had not exaggerated.

'Everybody late tonight?' asked Dawlish amiably.

'Late!' Pierpont spread his hands. 'Dinner in rooms, dinner in rooms, that is all I hear the whole evening. The patrons are frightened, Captain Dawlish, frightened; and who can blame them? At lunch it was bad, but not so bad as this.'

'They're crazy,' said Dawlish.

'Perhaps – but I repeat that they are frightened.'

'Particularly those who have nothing to be afraid of,' said Dawlish tartly.

But Pierpont went on: 'The name that this will give to my hotel – it is tragic, Captain Dawlish! And poor Frederick and his wife – what have I done that this should happen?'

Dawlish said: 'It won't last for ever.'

'One week, and my hotel is finished,' declared Pierpont.

Sympathy for Pierpont kept the others silent for a while, nor did they linger over their meal.

For an hour or more they sat in one of the lounges, but Dawlish was clearly on edge, and presently he and Felicity went out. Crummy had gone to relieve Ted or Tim, and Lockwood was with his wife.

'And now what?' asked Felicity a little grimly.

'We're going to see Eileen,' said Dawlish. 'I'll explain more in the car, my sweet.' Twice police guards stopped him before he left the grounds, and another patrol was watching the road.

'They're taking no chances,' said Felicity. 'How *can* Cole get through, even if he wants to?'

'That's precisely what I'm thinking,' admitted Dawlish. 'Some relaxation is indicated, we want to stop him getting out, not getting in. However, we can worry about that when we see Woodley. For the time being –'

He told her what he had reasoned about the actual activity of Raymond Black and Eileen. In the darkness of the car, just able to make out the vague outlines of his profile, she smiled a little.

'And the next plan?'

'To take Eileen for a ride! Actually, we could do with a better night than we've got, but it will have to serve. When we get to Winchester,' he added, 'there should be a map delivered by special messenger from the Yard. It will show all the places where there's been trouble on the farms. We're going to take Eileen to those within, say, a forty or fifty mile radius of the Lodge, and see if she can recognise any of them as places where she's been before.'

Felicity's eyes widened.

'That *is* an idea, Pat.'

'It should help,' said Dawlish, slowing down to avoid a cyclist wobbling in the middle of the road. 'Of course, she might not be able to identify anything. On the other hand, if she does, it very nearly clinches my argument.'

They reached Winchester police station some hours after darkness had fallen. Woodley was in his office, and the map had just been received. As it was addressed to Dawlish, he did not know what it was.

Dawlish explained a little.

Woodley was taken aback.

'So that's the business. I'd assumed that it was espionage, though I'd no idea it touched us so closely in this neighbourhood. We've been trying to stop these farm fires and the general damage for a long time, and we've sent a host of reports to Whitehall. How widespread is it?'

'Too wide to be comfortable,' said Dawlish. He went on to explain what he proposed to do, and a few minutes afterwards he was taken to Eileen.

A small room at the top of the police headquarters had been put aside for her, and she had been treated with every possible respect and consideration. But it was clear enough that she was harassed and on edge. She jumped up from her chair when Dawlish entered, her breathing quick and laboured.

'Oh – thank heavens you've come. Why are they keeping me here?'

Dawlish said easily: 'Now don't worry, Eileen. As for what you're doing here, you must blame me. I thought it the safest place for you.'

'Safest? I – but Raymond,' she added swiftly. 'Where is he? Why isn't he here?'

Dawlish said slowly: 'Eileen, I'm not going to lie, and I don't think there's any need to beat about the bush. Raymond is with Cole – '

'He's alive?'

'Of course he's alive,' said Dawlish. 'He's far too valuable to Colonel Cole for anything to happen to him.' He did not believe that, of course, but he had to comfort the girl, and he had to get her in the frame of mind most necessary for the night's exploration. 'Before we get hold of Cole, we need proof of what he's been doing. In helping us in this, you will be helping Raymond and yourself. We're going to visit the country over which you and Raymond have driven at night, and whenever we get to any place you recognise, I want you to tell us.'

'It – it won't be easy in the black-out.'

'It's usually been dark when you've driven.'

'Ye-es. Oh, yes, of course I'll do it, when do we start?'

'Right now,' said Dawlish.

He arranged with Woodley for a police car to go ahead

of him in the borrowed Austin; the driver was to follow the map which had been sent down from the Yard. They started off ten minutes later, but it was nearly an hour before Eileen said quickly:

'I remember this bridge, with the white paint and the red reflectors.' The driver ahead slowed down and then stopped. Dawlish followed suit, and Eileen climbed out of the car. They could make out the outline of a bar, and hear the slow movements of cattle in a nearby field. Two tall trees grew by the barn.

Eileen said sharply: 'Yes, we've been here. I remember those trees.'

'That's item one,' said Dawlish, and they drove on, stopping again half-an-hour later. The police driver said:

'They had a fire here only three weeks ago, sir.'

Eileen said: 'We – we were here about a month ago. I remember those four haystacks; they're round, not square.' She pointed to the stacks.

They travelled for over three hours about the countryside, and only at four of nine different stops was Eileen unable to be sure whether she had seen the places before. At the others there was always something by which she could identify the barns and the farmhouses, and there remained no reasonable doubt that Dawlish was right.

CHAPTER 31

No Doubt at All

There was no room for doubt.

In Dawlish's mind as they drove to Ringwood there was something approaching exhilaration. There were questions still to be answered, but the main point was proved, and the way in which the damage had been organised was now clear.

Woodley received the news with an enthusiasm as great as Dawlish's, while Dawlish pulled a telephone towards him, and after twenty minutes was connected with the London home of Sir Archibald Morely. Morely sounded sleepy, but that did not last for long. He listened in silence, then his voice came, sharp and alert.

'You're absolutely certain, Pat?'

'There's no doubt at all.'

'Then I'm coming down. Cole hasn't returned yet, you say . . . we'll hope that you're right and he *does* turn up, but we'll get him sooner or later, even if we don't get him this time. Now, Pat, there's another thing. I sent a messenger down with all the information I could get together about Cole. It should be at Winchester by now. Look through it. It bears out all we've thought about him being the last man to do this kind of thing – he's been one of the foremost anti-Nazi agitators for years.'

'That's not surprising,' said Dawlish.

'Eh?'

'I just said it wasn't surprising.'

'It is to me. The mentality of the German or the pro-German doesn't make it possible for him to do or say anything against the all-powerful Hitler.'

'Cole's a bit more subtle than that.'

'I'll take your word. Still, look through the papers, Pat – and I'll be down in about three hours. Leave word at the Lodge for me if you're not there.'

He rang off, and then Woodley telephoned to Winchester, to find that the second package for Dawlish had arrived. Woodley gave instructions for it to be sent immediately to the Lodge.

It was nearly four o'clock before Dawlish and Felicity returned there. Dawlish arranged to be called at seven-thirty. Tea, brought by May, greeted him on waking, and a few minutes afterwards Morely came into his room. Morely looked fresh and wideawake despite his short night, and was a little put out to find that so far Dawlish had done nothing about the dossier on Cole.

'Cole's not returned, Woodley tells me,' added the Assistant Commissioner.

'Oh, well,' said Dawlish, pouring out tea. 'Shall I send for another cup?'

'No thanks, Pierpont got me some breakfast as soon as I arrived.'

'Good,' said Dawlish, and began to scan Colonel Cole's record.

It was certainly a praiseworthy one. Some two years before the outbreak of war he had urged the need for putting agriculture in the country on a war footing, and immediately after the declaration of hostilities he had taken a leading, but always unofficial, part in the establishment of a first-class farmers' organisation in the three counties. He was a man of considerable wealth, and he himself owned a dozen farms, four of which had been seriously affected by fires just before harvest, and one made insolvent by an outbreak of foot-and-mouth disease involving the destruction of nearly a hundred head of cattle.

'That in itself would argue against Cole's complicity,' said Morely.

Dawlish raised an eyebrow.

'You're all for Cole, aren't you? Actually, he owns the

farms, he doesn't work them, and his capital isn't in them.'

'That's where you're wrong,' said Morely, with a certain air of triumph. 'If you'd read through that dossier you would see it. He's financed most of his tenants, and he's put a lot of money into other farms.'

Dawlish looked up sharply.

'*What* was that?'

'He's advanced considerable sums of money – I don't care what you say, Pat, but on the surface there's no reason at all for suspecting Cole, and but for your assurance I shouldn't believe anything against him. He's involved up to nearly a hundred thousand pounds. With each fire, each outbreak, he stands to lose more. And as he's persistently refused to take any official status, he has no salary, although he devotes all of his time to the work.'

'Well, well, well,' said Dawlish. 'That supplies the missing piece.'

Morely eyed him in bewilderment.

'What do you mean – what supplies it?'

'Cole's financial interest in the farms. How wide-spread is that interest? Just local, or – '

'It covers a wide area – a hundred thousand is a lot of money in land investment.'

'How substantial is Cole's capital?'

'It's not easy to say, but it's definitely less than it was. He held blocks of Bulgarian and Rumanian companies, and of course they're practically valueless at the moment. But he's financially sound, or he couldn't continue with what he's doing.'

'Well, well,' said Dawlish. 'He's lost heavily since the German putsch in the Balkans. He always knew that he would lose heavily there – anyone who had a ha'porth of common sense would. Now we're beginning to see the frame-work of Colonel Cole's little scheme, Archie.'

'Will you put that in plainer words?' asked Morely coldly.

'Of course. He's not worth all the money you think he is. In fact it could be that he's very nearly desperate for money. It gives me the answer to the one question I've been asking myself since Drew changed his attitude in a matter of seconds.'

'Now, come,' said Morely. 'I've been at pains to show you that Cole's invested considerable sums of money in land and in backing farmers, and if you're right, then he's destroying the yield which he might expect. Would any man sink his money into something which he is trying to ruin? Of course,' went on Morely thoughtfully, 'if he's receiving money from Berlin, that does make it more understandable. The only thing is that nothing in Cole's past record suggests that he's prepared to work against us. When he was in the army he was one of the fire-eaters – in the last war he had a grudge because we didn't go on to Berlin. He's always advocated that only a partitioned Germany will be kept from making war. At the time of the Austrian *anschluss* he made himself extremely unpopular with the Conservative Party for advocating military action against Hitler. In fact he lost a "safe" seat in the House because of it. He –'

Dawlish poured himself another cup of tea.

'What you're trying to tell me is that you think it could be a case of mistaken identity – is that it?'

Morely said: 'Couldn't it be?'

'No. I've seen Cole several times. He's got a profile I couldn't mistake, I'm quite sure of that. The one outside possibility is that Cole has been impersonated at the Manor for some time, but I don't believe it's likely. Colonel Cole, the real Cole, is the man behind this business. I'll stake my life on it.'

Morely shrugged.

'All right, Pat. I'm not going to argue with you. I know you wouldn't talk so definitely without reason; but it doesn't make sense whichever way you look at it. Either Cole had a complete *volte face*, turning from a bitter anti-Nazi to a pro-Nazi, working with them and taking their money, or he's ruining himself.'

'Wrong, both ways,' said Dawlish.

'*What?*'

'I said "wrong, both ways", and I still think you are,'

said Dawlish, flinging the bedclothes back and stretching out for his bath-robe. 'The whole thing has been cock-eyed from the beginning. I saw it the same way as you did, at first. But I stopped when Drew changed so oddly. I've told you fully about that, and warned you that Drew's an essential witness. He's all right, I hope?'

'Yes, he's at a hospital near Staines, and strongly guarded.'

'Good,' said Dawlish. 'I –'

He stopped as the door opened abruptly, and Ted Beresford came in. About him there was an air of excitement and no suggestion at all that his night's rest had been a mere three hours. He stormed into the room, clapped Morely heavily on the shoulder, and beamed at Dawlish.

'What, tea at this hour of the morning? Shame on you. Well, old chap, you're right again. He's back.'

Morely repeated faintly: '*He's back?*'

'Well, well, well!' exclaimed Pat Dawlish. 'So the Colonel's on his own premises. For how long?'

'He got there twenty minutes ago, in a closed car. We saw him entering the Manor – Tim and I were up a tree,' explained Beresford, as if it was a natural occurrence. 'And he had an oldish woman with him – Felicity's charmer, I wouldn't be surprised. The car's still standing outside the door.'

'Well – I'm – damned!' exclaimed Morely.

'We took the more ostentatious guards away, word reached Cole, and he comes back,' said Dawlish slowly. 'It had to be – he had to get hold of his records, and he keeps them at the Manor. He has one chance of fighting, and that's from the Manor. I don't think I'll shave this morning.'

'Going straight there?' asked Morely.

'I don't know,' said Dawlish. 'I may not need to.'

'But –'

'He may come here,' said Dawlish, and he laughed a little. 'He has good friends at the Lodge – friends who have committed murder for him and would put Cole's safety and cause before all other things. So Cole will want to contact them. They'll either go to Cole, or he'll come here.'

'Are you *crazy?*' demanded Morely.

'That suggestion again?' asked Dawlish reproachfully. 'No, I'm not crazy. I don't think it's possible for a man to disguise himself so well that he would be mistaken by old acquaintances for Colonel Cole, but I do think Cole's capable of adopting a disguise which would make him look unlike himself. D'you follow?'

'Yes. But why should he come here?'

Dawlish paused above a hand-basin filled with cold water.

'Because he went to the Manor, and let himself be seen. He knows that we now know he's at the Manor. He'll expect us to rush all our forces there – and then he'll come here. It doesn't matter much how he makes the journey, but through the woods and then across the shrubberies to appear in the grounds of the Lodge as a resident whom no one suspects, is my guess.'

'Unless he was seen in the woods.'

'A hotel resident wouldn't be stopped by any of the guards. Supposing Cole comes out of the Manor as Cole, and goes into the woods. While the guards are looking for him, he changes his clothes and adds, perhaps, a moustache, or a wig. He bobs up again some distance from where he changes, and the guards see a Lodge resident. They might question him, but as he's "not" Cole, they'd probably let him go through, merely reporting that he'd been seen. It's simple, and it's likely to succeed because it's daring. From the start I've seen the connection between the Lodge and the Manor. I could see no possible reason, for instance, for the murder of Smith, unless he'd seen something dangerous. And I think Smith was known to be watching Raymond Black, and saw something at the window which made his murder imperative. Supposing he saw Cole with Black? Or supposing – '

He broke off, for again the door opened abruptly, and this time it was Felicity who entered. She said quickly:

'Pat, Black's coming into the Lodge! I've just seen him from the window.'

195

'So he got away!' exclaimed Ted Beresford.

'Don't you believe it!' said Dawlish. 'Where are my trousers? He didn't get away – Archie, there's your resident, the man Cole can impersonate. Dress Cole in padded clothes, and he's thickset. Let him dress in clothes that aren't padded, and he's thin. We've never seen Black and Cole together, mind you.'

Felicity said:

'You mean to say that Black *is* Cole?'

'Let's say Cole is Black – on occasions,' grinned Dawlish. 'Let's assume also that Smith saw enough at the window to realise it. Let's go to see our Raymond.'

'But – but Eileen?'

'Possibly a clever little girl,' said Dawlish. 'Where's my collar?' He was dressing swiftly as he talked. 'Perhaps a very clever little girl, our Eileen; but still could be innocent of the darker crimes.'

He opened the door, fastening his belt about him as he walked along the passage, the others in his wake. He reached the head of the stairs as Black came up them. Black looked very pale – too pale to be natural, thought Dawlish. His clothes were dishevelled, but his hair was neatly parted, an odd thing.

Dawlish pulled up, as if in surprise.

'Black what the devil – '

'I must talk to you,' said Raymond Black urgently. 'It's important Dawlish. I managed to get away. Cole – Cole's over at the Manor. I've just come from there. He's preparing a sortie – he's destroying incriminating papers, and then he's going to try to drive out – the car has two machine-guns in it, and Stenner's there with another man. They – ' he stopped, and brushed a hand across his forehead. 'They're desperate, Dawlish – '

'Yes, they would be,' said Patrick Dawlish, and he was smiling widely. 'But only one man of Cole's height has gone into the Manor in the past twenty-four hours, Black. And according to what you say, you've just come from there. One moment – ' he reached forward as Black stepped back, and pulled at the neatly arranged hair.

It came off.

Then the man who had presented himself as Raymond Black kicked out, sent Dawlish staggering back, turned, and rushed down the stairs.

CHAPTER 32

Nearly the End

It was unfortunate that Morely and Beresford had been crowding Dawlish. He lost precious seconds in recovering his balance. Footsteps thundered down the stairs as he snapped out:

'Ted, climb out of a window, and get police and anyone you find in the grounds. Morely, you'd better go with Ted –'

The two men hurried to the window at the end of the passage. Felicity raced in the wake of Dawlish, and they reached the ground floor together. Two or three residents were standing there, wide-eyed.

'Get out of the hall!' snapped Dawlish. He heard Cole's voice from the domestic part of the hotel, and he caught two names – names which should have surprised him, but somehow did not. He heard doors closing, and he saw a startled policeman turning from an equally startled woman receptionist.

Dawlish spoke to the policeman:

'Keep everybody out of the hall – get them into one of the lounges. Don't ask questions, do it!'

He went towards the domestic quarters, and then he stopped, for he saw Cole again, and behind Cole he saw Pierpont and Millsham – *and all three men held guns.*

*

He wished then that he had made Felicity stay upstairs. That was the main thought in his mind. He said quickly:

'Get down behind the desk, sweetheart,' and then he pressed the trigger of his revolver. Millsham took the bullet, and staggered backwards, but Cole came on. Dawlish saw a heavy settee, and leapt for it.

The movement nonplussed the three men. Millsham had recovered, temporarily at least, and was making for the open front door.

Dawlish nudged the settee a few inches further from the wall, and was able to train his gun on Pierpont, but as he did so Cole fired. The bullet caught the side of the settee, and plunged through it.

Cole was now halfway to the door, where Millsham was keeping guard until the others joined him.

As Dawlish showed himself for a moment, Pierpont moved his gun round again. Dawlish's finger was on the trigger, and he fired a fraction of a second ahead of the hotelier! Pierpont took the bullet in the chest. He gasped, dropped the gun, then slowly crumpled to the floor.

Millsham and Cole had reached the steps.

There was a small car not thirty yards along the drive, and they began to race towards it, Millsham's left arm hanging uselessly. Dawlish fired twice, missing by a fraction each time. An attempt to fire a third time proved useless; the gun was empty.

He started to run, hurrying after his quarry. Several men were converging on the car, but none were as near as Cole and Millsham.

Quickly Dawlish reloaded and took careful aim. He saw Millsham stagger, but the bullet did not stop the man altogether. He was about to fire again when he heard a shout from Felicity:

'Look out – your right!'

He glanced quickly to the right, and then he saw a strange thing – an oldish woman, grey-haired and clad in a fashion fifty years behind the time, was climbing through the window of one of the lounges. She had an automatic in her right hand, and it was levelled towards Dawlish. Instinctively he swerved. He did not see the bullet, but he felt the wind of it as it passed his face. A stone hurtled through the air, breaking a window, and he guessed that it was flung by Felicity.

The woman fired again, but missed, and a second stone, following the first, reached its target, and the woman toppled over.

Dawlish went on towards the car.

Cole was at the wheel, Millsham was climbing over the side. The engine started, missed, then started again. A dozen men were now converging on the car. Bullets whanged against its wings, the windscreen was pierced at least twice. But Cole was not hit, or at least not badly wounded, and the car was already moving fast towards the drive gates. It was impossible for Dawlish to keep up with it, or halt its progress. Cole was driving like a man possessed, swaying the car from side to side to make a more difficult target. The grounds of the Lodge were like a rifle-range, echoing and re-echoing to the crack of bullets, while the shouting of the men and the roar of the engine added to the din.

Felicity reached Dawlish's side.

'They can't make it,' she said.

'No-o?' said Dawlish slowly, and then more definitely: 'No, they can't. But they'll try to the limit. And unless someone's had the sense to close the gates, they might get through and do a lot more damage before we get 'em.' He stood quite still, his lips set, his chin thrust forward.

And then he snapped:

'Great Scott, look!'

The little car had reached the gates, and as it did so, a larger car turned into the drive. There was no chance at all for either driver to pull up.

Felicity said in a low voice:

'Tim's Bentley.'

'Ye-es – ' Dawlish's voice was hardly audible. There was no time to think, time only to watch. And although it happened very quickly, the split-second between the first glimpse of the car and the moment of impact seemed to take an age. He could see Tim and Crummy in the Bentley, both obviously prepared to jump. The little car swerved to one side as the Bentley seemed to leap into the air.

Tim and Crummy jumped.

The larger car, quite out of control, reared above the other – and then the crash came.

To Dawlish, it was like something seen in a film, yet the sight and the sound of it spurred him into action, and he began to run. Quickly as he went, half-a-dozen other men were there before him. Ted Beresford was bending over Tim, and a policeman was kneeling by Crummy Wise.

Dawlish reached Tim.

'He's all right,' Ted said crisply. 'Knocked out, but nothing broken as far as I can see.'

'Thank the Lord for that,' said Dawlish fervently, and then he stepped round the wreckage to Crummy. Crummy was conscious and grinning, but his right leg was bent in an odd fashion.

'No pain,' he croaked, 'so don't fuss.'

Dawlish lit a cigarette and handed it to him.

'What brought you?'

'We saw Black come out, and started to think,' said Crummy. 'Then we reasoned that Black couldn't have got in after Cole's disappearance since the place had been watched, so it was odd that he could come out. Then we thought that Cole had gone in, and Black had come out. They measured right in height, and –' he grinned more widely – 'then there was a puff of wind, and we got wise to the wig. After that –'

'*Ve*-ry nice work,' said Dawlish easily. 'We reached the conclusion about the same time, then. Tim's all right, and the casualties aren't too numerous.'

'Fine,' said Crummy Wise. 'Then that's the end of a nice bunch of spies!'

Morely had come from behind Dawlish, and he said slowly:

'I still don't follow it all.'

'That's easy,' said Crummy. 'One nest of spies, working at the Lodge and the Manor. What's a better place for a rendezvous than a quiet country hotel run by a respectable cove like Pierpont? They – spies, I mean – could come and go more or less as they pleased. Isn't that so, Pat?'

Dawlish looked thoughtful.

'They *could* have done all that. The question is, did they? I don't think there's a spy angle in this show at all. I haven't done since Drew changed his manner so oddly.'

Crummy's face dropped.

'What? No spies?'

'No spies, or that's my guess,' said Patrick Dawlish. 'But I'll tell you what we find when you've had your leg set. Until then, be patient. Let's see the others, Archie, shall we?'

Morely said slowly:

'Millsham's dead – the doctor fellow. Black – or Cole – is alive but badly hurt. I don't think he'll live long. But Pat – do you seriously mean that it's *not* espionage?'

'That's my bet,' said Dawlish; and then they went to the side of Colonel Cole, who had called himself for a time by another name.

CHAPTER 33

What Spies?

The man was conscious, but it was clear that he had little chance of recovery. He seemed to realise that himself. His face, a short while before set in such raging fury, was drawn and haggard, yet showed no enmity. His lips curled a little when Dawlish approached him.

His voice was clear but weak.

'So you rumbled me, Dawlish?'

'Not until pretty late,' said Dawlish quietly. 'How are your feeling?'

'I don't feel much, and I hope I won't again. If – if I get a lot of pain, shoot some morphia into me. Will you do that?'

'Yes,' said Dawlish.

'Thanks – I – '

'I hope you'll make a full statement,' said Morely.

'Yes, I will. It makes no odds, since you've got us all. Drew's still a prisoner?'

'Yes.'

'So there isn't one of us left,' said Cole, speaking very slowly. 'When you came, Dawlish. I thought you were just a loud-mouthed fool, out to get showy results. I didn't think you'd get me.'

'I nearly didn't,' said Dawlish.

'What use is – nearly? I – I don't mind much. It's been a strain, a dreadful strain. I couldn't face – the financial loss. The – the disasters in Rumania – Bulgaria. I've been insolvent for six months.' He was silent for a few minutes, then went on, his voice weaker, but no less resolute.

'I prepared this – this racket. Drew had had experience – gang experience. Millsham and Pierpont found out about it, and muscled in.' Another smile twisted the dying man's lips. 'Black – a German, hiding the fact, scared of admitting it – gave me the idea. He did the work for me. Put acid in corn and seed stocks. Caused foot-and-mouth – taking parts of tainted beasts to water troughs at other farms –' Cole paused, and drew a sharp breath. 'You'll remember that morphia, won't you?'

'Yes,' said Dawlish, and he turned to a man standing near. 'Fetch Dr Millsham's case from his room, please.' He looked back at Cole, who nodded as if in thanks, and then went on with an obvious effort:

'Black didn't know – what he was doing. Believed the robbery story. So did – so did his girl. Dawlish, don't let her have trouble. She's lied to you, for Black. I told her he'd be killed if she didn't. Don't –'

'She'll be all right,' said Dawlish.

Cole's breath was coming in shorter gasps, and Dawlish wiped perspiration from his forehead. 'I – I can't understand myself, now. I was driven crazy for want of money. I'd none – had heavy mortgages everywhere. Then Pierpont and Millsham offered to finance the scheme – my doing, my idea, their money. Buy ground – lend money on mortgages to farmers – break the farmers by ruining their stocks, and close down on them. Thus getting the land for a quarter of its value. Get – get the idea?'

Morely said: 'Dawlish got it some time back.'

'Did he now. Smarter than I thought. Well, that's it. We've got a third of Hampshire, nearly as much of the other two counties – all ready for taking. This harvest – if bad – would smash – hundreds of farmers. But the land would be twice, three times its pre-war value. I would have the title to it. The Government would subsidise the actual farmers, but the land was mine. I worked on some of my own farms, to make sure I wasn't suspected. I –' he stopped again.

'I'll go on,' said Dawlish quietly. 'There isn't much more,

of course. You had the title to all of this land, and you were quite free to develop it, and to make what terms you liked. You could deal with the Government as an independent agent, that's why you always worked unofficially, and accepted no Government office.'

Cole nodded.

'We'll get to the last day or two,' said Dawlish. 'Smith saw you in the room as Black – you took your wig off – right?'

Another nod.

'You had to get rid of him quickly. You couldn't do it as yourself, and you didn't want Black suspected – the real Black. So you borrowed my uniform, knowing I was about your size, killed Smith, and then went back to the Manor. Eileen made it appear that only Black had been in her room all the time. That's why you made Black share a room with her, why you made them put on the married act. You wanted to have an alibi for all emergencies, so that you could go in and out of the Lodge as Black.'

'Ye-es.'

'Then you learned of Prior. You found he suffered from headaches, and you substituted the poison tablets. You believed he was silenced before he could talk. You warned me, not knowing I was *ex-officio* with the police. You and your lady-friend worked the trick on Felicity, to try to scare me off. You had the cake-shop in Ringwood as a secondary cover – if anything was traced to this part of the country, then the cake-shop was to be "revealed" as the headquarters. You kept the men – Drew's men – there. Is that right?'

Again Cole nodded.

'Who is the lady-friend?'

'An old servant – of Millsham's.'

'I see. And now to Frederick. He knew Pierpont was up to some funny business, and he was dangerous. So was his wife. You shot the wife, not by mistake but because of what she knew, and Fred realised who had done it, and was out for vengeance. You – '

'Not me. Millsham. Millsham shot them both, making it look like murder and suicide. I didn't know about that until they phoned me, yesterday. At Roehampton – just before you arrived. There – there isn't much more, Dawlish.'

'Just oddments,' said Dawlish, and he looked round as a man came up. Morely said:

'Do you want a shot of morphia, Cole?'

'In – in a minute –' he drew a deep breath, and grimaced. 'That girl, Eileen. Look after her. And Black – Black's in the Ley Farm Cottage. Gave me a – a perfect cover. Lent a spy-angle to it all – no one would ever suspect me of spying.' He lapsed into silence, and then said in a wandering voice: 'Spies? What spies?'

*

Colonel Cole died ten minutes later, and it was not long before the final steps were taken to clear up the affair which had proved to be so different from what it had first appeared. The real Raymond Black, or Bache, told Dawlish and the others that he had first started to take Cole's orders a year before. He had not known that, on occasions, Cole had impersonated him. It was clear to Dawlish that Cole had wanted to make sure that he was not personally suspected, so, in order to keep in closer touch with Pierpont and Millsham, he had planned to adopt Black's identity when necessary.

Black himself had at first kept silent, but after the visit to London he had decided he could not go on with it, and had returned to tell Dawlish the truth. After Dawlish had left him at the flat, with Stenner, two other men had come in, and he had been forced to leave. The men who had been sent from the Yard to watch were found, that day, badly injured in an empty flat not far from Dawlish's. How they had been lured from their post was simple enough; they had been given a message purporting to come from Dawlish, and had gone to the flat, where they were afterwards found, to make inquiries. There they had been attacked.

'One way and the other it was a clever show,' said Dawlish

later that evening. 'Drew was the operating member – the man of action, so to speak. I doubt if you'll get him to talk, but you've got enough on him to have him hanged.'

'More than enough,' agreed Morely.

'And what of Eileen Granger?' asked Dawlish.

'She'll be all right,' Morely assured him. 'She acted under duress. Black will be interned, but that won't last for ever. Seeing how things have turned out, we won't be vindictive towards him.'

'I should hope not!' said Patrick Dawlish with feeling. 'But for Black I doubt whether we should have got where we did anything like as quickly.'

'There's one thing I haven't seen yet,' said Morely. 'Why were you so sure that it wasn't espionage after Drew – according to the others – admitted that it was?'

Dawlish smiled.

'Archie, it shouts at you. Drew had all the courage you could expect from a man, but when we suggested spying he became a craven. On the "you-know-all" principle. I took it from that that he *wanted* me to continue to believe that, and so conversely I assumed it wasn't true. The Black angle grew obvious then. Well, I'm glad they'll get through, bless their hearts. Is there anything else?'

'No,' said Morely, and he smiled a little grimly. 'Not this time.'

Dawlish left the Yard, and then went to his flat, where Ted and Tim – Tim suffering no more than a bump on the head – and Felicity were waiting. There was good news of Crummy, whose injuries had not been severe, so that there was cause for general satisfaction.

Felicity, who could do miracles with scanty rations, prepared a meal; and there was beer. Afterwards Dawlish lit his pipe, and Felicity sat on his knee, while Ted Beresford said:

'It was a good show, Pat, but you were infernally mysterious half of the time.'

'Far too mysterious,' concurred Tim.

Dawlish raised one eyebrow above the other.

'There's no point in sending everyone haring up the wrong tree when with a little patience one can spot the right one. The trouble with you people is that you never know when to be grateful. We'll all be able to get another week's leave out of this, and what more can you want?'

'Not a thing,' said Felicity happily.

THE END